Tell Me Tomorrow and Other Stories

Karen Clark

authorHOUSE®

AuthorHouse™ UK
1663 Liberty Drive
Bloomington, IN 47403 USA
www.authorhouse.co.uk
Phone: UK TFN: 0800 0148641 (Toll Free inside the UK)
        UK Local: (02) 0369 56322 (+44 20 3695 6322 from outside the UK)

Published by AuthorHouse 11/19/2021

ISBN: 978-1-6655-9462-2 (sc)
ISBN: 978-1-6655-9461-5 (e)

Print information available on the last page.

CONTENTS

TELL ME TOMORROW

"**M**aria, are you coming?" called Ann, as her workmate lingered by the door, her mind completely elsewhere.

"Oh - yes; won't be a moment," Maria replied, hurriedly placing her overalls into her locker, before joining Ann in the corridor leading to the exit of the school.

"Thank God it's Friday," breathed Ann with a sigh of relief, as they made their way to reception, glad that, at last, the weekend was waiting in the wings. "I bet you can't wait for the concert tomorrow; will Mike be able to make it there, after all? It'll be a waste of a ticket if he *can't.*"

"Yes," said Maria with a smile, as they came to the foyer and bid the receptionist goodbye. "He's picking me up at two fifteen."

"Can I ask a favour?" struck in Ann, as they exited reception, stepping out into the mild, summer air. "Can Mike give *me* a lift to the concert hall, too? I've a cheek, haven't I?"

"No," Maria sheepishly replied, too polite to agree with her bold, pushy friend who cadged lifts quite a lot.

Ann pressed the green button beside the double doors, which opened with a click; the two women stepping outside towards the grey, metallic gates separating the pavement from the school.

"Would 3 o' clock be OK - by the clock tower and fountains in 'Pepper Mill Road?'" Maria asked, as they walked through the gates and headed for the bus stop at the end of the road.

"The concert doesn't start until seven," said Ann with a frown, as they reached the stop and sat down on its plastic, red bench.

"Mike and I will be going to "Pepper Mill's Café" for a bite to eat before the concert begins," Maria mildly replied, wondering why Ann could not make her way to the concert by herself. "You could join us, if you like."

"It's a deal," agreed Ann, as they saw their bus come. "Certainly beats sitting in the car."

The bus pulled up at the stop, swinging open its doors as Maria and Ann climbed aboard, plumping for the seat opposite the stairs that led to the empty upper deck.

"It'll be the school summer holidays soon; me and Jake are taking a vacation as soon as they're here," said Ann, smiling with glee; the school submerging as the bus began to move, going round a corner at the lights as they turned emerald green.

"Where will you be going?" Maria asked, checking her pockets for the key to the door of their abode.

"Milan," said her housemate with a grin. "Jake wanted to go to New York - but I wasn't keen."

Maria lowered her eyes, as the bus stopped again; its doors swinging open once more to admit more passengers on board. As the doors re-shut, they heard the sound of footsteps from below, growing louder with each second that passed, as a familiar male figure emerged, flashing the two women a welcoming grin.

"Mike!" exclaimed Ann in surprise. "I thought you were at work. What on earth are you doing on the bus at *this* time of day?"

"I took the afternoon off; I'm going into town to buy myself an outfit for tonight," replied Mike, casually positioning himself in the opposite seat.

"Oh, the concert!" Ann opportunely cut in; her eyes lighting up. "That reminds me; Maria's said you wouldn't mind picking me up at "Pepper Mill Road" for a bite to eat with you both at 3 o' clock - and then we can all make our way to the concert together."

"I suppose we *could* squeeze you in," Mike replied, doubting if Ann would be paying her share of the bill.

"Oh, bless you, Mike; you're a gem!" exclaimed Ann, as Mike threw his girlfriend an uncertain glance, wishing that they had discussed Ann's request before he had 'agreed' to oblige.

"Anyway, what kind of outfit do you have in mind to buy?" asked Maria at last, seizing her opportunity to speak.

"Batman? Superman? The Incredible Hulk?" Ann jokingly enquired.

"Don't be daft; I need to look smart - or I may not be let into the hall," answered Mike, as the bus abandoned the stop, whizzing through streets that were growing more grey and built-up.

"Is it a surprise?" Maria curiously asked. "Are we not supposed to know until tomorrow?"

"Not really," said Mike with a shrug, bracing himself for another facetious remark from her bold, pushy friend. "I've been meaning to buy some new clothes for myself for some time - but never got round to it. I'm after blue denims, a grey checked shirt and a jacket to match—and while I'm visiting the stores, I'll hunt out a suit for the office, as well."

"Oh, look; there's our stop; we'd better get off," cut in Ann, as the bus slowed its speed, ready to grind to a halt.

"I hope you find the clothes that you want," said Maria to Mike, who gave her hand an affectionate squeeze before she and Ann rose from their seats and made for the stairs.

"See you at your lodgings tomorrow at a quarter past two," called Mike to Maria, as he lingered in his seat, watching his girlfriend and Ann swiftly submerge from the top of the stairs before getting off the bus.

As the bus drove away, Maria looked round, returning Mike's wave from the street before he submerged.

"Damn!" said Ann with a sigh, as she and Maria crossed the road, heading for the house that they shared. "My keys are trapped at the bottom of my bag, and I can't get them out. Would you mind if we used yours?"

"OK," said Maria as they reached the front door of their rented abode, wishing she could afford a flat of her own. "They're in my pocket; I'll get them out," she added, as the door suddenly swung open before she could oblige.

"Maria! Ann! Come in!" cried the amiable voice that emerged from the hall.

"Lara - what are *you* doing back here so soon?" exclaimed Ann, as she and Maria stepped through the door and into the hall.

"I had the afternoon off work," Lara replied, as the three housemates made their way into the large, communal lounge and sat down on the couch.

"We've just met Mike on the bus; *he* had the afternoon off work today, as well." Maria declared, as she and Ann took off their jackets, placing them over their laps in a slovenly way.

"Yes, I know. He was going into town to buy some new clothes," Lara said with a grin.

"And what will *you* wear for the concert tomorrow?" Ann curiously probed.

"Nothing special," Lara casually replied. "*Maria's* the biggest Ray Silverton fan - so I'm sure it will be *she* who'll dress up to the nines; am I right, Maria?" she asked, shifting her blue, saucer eyes to Ann's taciturn friend.

"Yes - my green, satin leggings and glittery top," Maria said; her tone composed, but her eyes excited and keen.

"Oh - snazzy! Is there any dazzling jewellery to match?" Lara cried; she and Ann swapping looks.

4

Before Maria could reply, the ring of the doorbell from the passage hit everyone's ears, before Lara got up from the couch and made for the door.

"I'd better go and see who that is," she said, disappearing from the room.

"That's Jake; he's come for me early," said Ann to Maria, recognizing her boyfriend's voice from the doorstep beyond.

"Will you two be staying out late?" Maria asked, as they heard the front door click shut.

"Not as late as we'll all be staying out *tomorrow* night, I suppose," Ann emphatically replied, as the door of the lounge re-opened, making way for the entrance of Lara and Jake.

"*You're* early, Jake," remarked Ann. "Don't tell me *you* had the afternoon off work, as well."

"I guess *none of us* can concentrate on work right now," Jake dryly replied. "Tomorrow's concert is far more exciting than boring, old work. And I'm sorry I can't drop you to the concert hall tomorrow; I have to visit Joe - but I reckon I'll be able to make it there just about in time."

"Don't worry," Ann sullenly replied. "Mike said he'd give me and Maria a lift there tomorrow."

Jake threw his girlfriend a cautionary glance, as Maria and Lara uneasily lowered their eyes.

"That's why I've turned up here as early as I have," he told Ann, as the others in the room looked on. "—to spend the time that I won't be able to spend with you tomorrow - before the concert starts—and to treat you to a special afternoon in the centre of town."

"We're going into *town*?" Ann exclaimed with a smile. "I haven't been there for such a long time."

"I thought that would cheer you up," remarked Jake with a debonair grin. "So let's make our way there, and waste no more time."

"Hear that, Ann?" asked Lara in jest. "You're in for a nice surprise; it's your lucky day!"

"I suppose I *can* just about forgive you, then, Jake," Ann heedlessly said, slipping her jacket back on as she rose from the couch.

"You shall not be disappointed," said Jake, as he and Ann swiftly made for the door, leaving Lara and Maria on the couch.

"Bye," called Maria with a wave.

"Have fun," Lara said. "If I don't see you again tonight, I'll see you tomorrow evening at the hall."

"Bye!" Jake and Ann called, submerging from the lounge in a flash.

"Do you think Ann's still angry that Jake won't be going with her to the concert?" Maria asked, as Lara stretched out her arms, curling up her toes which she scanned with her circular eyes.

"I'm not sure," Lara said with a shrug. "As far as *I'm* concerned, Ann's problem's already been solved in that you and Mike will be giving her a lift instead of Jake," she coolly went on, realising Ann liked her own way a little too much.

Maria did not reply; she stared into Lara's blue eyes, waiting for her to say more. Lara's face broke into a smile; her expression warm and sincere.

"Don't worry about Ann; she can more than take care of herself. You must learn to think of *yourself* a bit more; no one *else* will," she finally resumed, exercising again as she sat on the couch.

Lara's words had hit a raw nerve; Maria throwing her a smile of subtle unease.

"You're right," Maria said, as she rose from the couch, "My self-esteem *is* a bit low."

"Forget about that!" Lara advised, in a light-hearted tone. "Forget about *everything* just now; just think about tomorrow's concert and the pleasure it will bring."

"Oh, I *am*," Maria stressfully replied, heading for the door of the lounge with her jacket in her grasp. "So much so that I'm going to my room to sort out what jewellery to wear with my leggings and top—and I *must* get hold of Mike while he's in town; hope his phone's switched on."

"Will you be coming down later for a brew" Lara asked, as Maria pulled open the door.

"I suppose," Maria replied, without having given her plans for the evening a thought.

"See you later, then, alligator," Lara purred, as Maria threw her a smile and exited the lounge, ascending the stairs in the hall that led to her room.

🕐 🕐 🕐 🕐 🕐

The fierce morning sun flooded the bedsit with light, as having slept very soundly last night, Maria woke up, feeling refreshed and ready to meet the new day. But this was to be no ordinary day; this was the day of the concert - an event which she had been eagerly awaiting for months.

She got out of bed and walked to the sink, turning on the taps to engage in her brief, morning wash. The clothes she would wear for the concert dazzled her eyes as they lay in the chair at the opposite end of the room; the sleek, satin leggings turning blue as they merged with the sun's golden rays.

Deciding against putting them on until just before Mike picked her up, Maria went over to the wardrobe to pull out her T-shirt and jeans. Moving her hand to open its teak, mirrored door, she sensed that something was wrong, as the mirror reflected a flat, rectangular object she had not seen before on the wall above the bed.

She turned round and walked back to the bed, scanning the area of wall where the object was pinned.

7

It was a poster; a snapshot of Ray Silverton occupying its bulk. As she took a closer look at her favourite star, he looked as if he had aged and that time had moved on. With a tentative breath, she slid her eyes from her idol's frame to the caption below, starting with shock as its words rudely sunk in:

"Ray Silverton," it read in bold letters that loudly stood out, below which featured the year he was born to the year he had died.

Maria sat down on the bed, raising her hand to her mouth in dismay at what she had seen; and on scouring her surroundings again, discovered that the shape of her room had changed from oblong to square.

It was only 6.30am - both by her watch and the clock by her bed, but already the wail of the kettle and clinking of cups met her ears from the kitchen downstairs.

"No way would I be able to sleep if I went back to bed," Maria uttered to herself, as she slipped off her nightdress and put on her T-shirt and jeans, wondering if Lara or Ann had placed the poster in her room - and why. Running a comb through her hair, she exited the room, descending the stairs that led to the hallway in haste. But as she entered the kitchen, eager to speak to Lara and Ann, two faces stared back - faces that she had never clapped eyes on before.

She froze in shock by the door, continuing to gaze at the faces she had not seen before. The strangers abruptly fell quiet, until one - a young woman in a red, floral dress, with long, auburn hair and steely blue eyes - finally shattered the ice.

"Maria, are you OK? You look as if you've just seen a ghost!" she exclaimed, in an unfamiliar voice.

Still lost for words, Maria remained transfixed on the faces in the room: how did these two young women know who she was?

"Where are Lara and Ann? We were all due to go to a concert tonight," she heard herself cry.

The two women exchanged puzzled looks, before eyeing Maria as if she were not making sense.

"The Ray Silverton concert?" asked the girl sitting next to her auburn-haired friend. "That was cancelled ages ago. I can't forget how devastated you were at the time - particularly after you heard the sad news," she went on, swapping looks with the auburn-haired girl once again.

"She was distraught, wasn't she, Kay?" said the auburn-haired girl to the other, whose hair was blonde and whose eyes were a light shade of brown.

"Absolutely, Fiona," the other acquiesced. "It was absolutely tragic the way Ray Silverton died."

Maria found herself stunned into silence once more; but her instincts cautioned her not to mention that - only the previous day - Ray Silverton was alive and the concert was due to go ahead.

"Come and sit down," Fiona said, leading Maria by the arm to the chair at the table facing her own. "Perhaps you're still half asleep, and so think Ray Silverton's still here. It's OK, Maria," she went on, patting Maria on the arm as they both took a seat. "It's hard to accept that the idol you've worshipped is gone."

Maria stayed quiet, waiting for Fiona or Kay to make the next move.

"Sit and relax for a while," Fiona advised, fetching Maria a mug of hot tea. "This should help you unwind."

"Thanks," said Maria, taking a sip from the mug, as Fiona sat back in her seat.

"We'll be going to 'Pepper Mill's Café' for lunch; do you want to come along?" Fiona asked with a sympathetic smile as she finished her toast. "It's always nice to have an outing at the weekend - even if it's only down the road."

9

So it was still a Saturday, then? At least *that* Maria had got right.

"Yes - that would be great," Maria lukewarmly replied, continuing to feel that nothing was real as she forced a faint smile.

Fiona got up, grabbing the empty plates which she placed in the sink at the end of the room.

"We'll see you in the lounge at 11 o' clock," she said to Maria as Kay abandoned her seat. "In the meantime, I must ring Keith to see if he's any plans for tonight. Try to relax, Maria - and we'll both see you soon."

"Yes, Maria - chill out," Kay advised, as she and Fiona exited the room, leaving Maria alone to wonder how she had woken up in an alien world.

🕐 🕐 🕐 🕐 🕐

As Kay pulled up on the corner of "Pepper Mill Road," Maria noticed that the clock tower looked different from before. It was now a silvery blue, and the face of its clock transformed from an insipid white to a stylish jet black, making its golden hands and numbers stand out.

"I'd better put some money in the metre," said Kay, thinking out loud, as she and her housemates unfastened their belts and got out of the car.

"Look, I know it must be hard - with you struggling to pay your share of the rent without work," said Fiona to Maria, whilst Kay plied the metre with change. "I'm sorry your job situation turned out the way it did - but something else will turn up. In the meantime, lunch is on us, so put away your purse," she added with a sympathetic smile, as Kay re-emerged with a grin, placing her money back in her bag as she, Fiona and Maria headed for "Pepper Mill's Café," which stood a few metres away.

As they reached the café entrance the clock tower struck

twelve, Maria feeling confused at what Fiona had said about her being out of a job – a job she had not been aware she no longer had. As Fiona opened the door and they all stepped inside, Maria saw that the café's interior had also been changed. Its walls were now pink, and framed pepper mill etchings hung neatly above each table in turn.

"There's hardly anyone here," Fiona observed, as they plumped for a table providing a view of the street.

"Good; that means we won't have a long wait before being served," Kay gleefully said, removing her coat which she placed at the back of the chair.

As the housemates ordered their meals, two customers came in, one a face that Maria knew very well. It was unmistakably Mike's, though he looked a bit older somehow, and his hair was now cropped. Accompanying him was a pretty, blonde girl of not more than nineteen. Maria saw Fiona and Kay exchanging uncomfortable looks as the couple emerged, arm in arm; Mike throwing the housemates a glance of unease before he and the girl took a seat at the furthest table they could find from Maria and her friends.

"Oh dear; perhaps inviting you to lunch at 'Pepper Mill's Café' *wasn't* such a good idea, after all," Fiona said to Maria with a sigh.

"We're sorry that you had to bump into Mike and his new girlfriend, when we'd meant to try and take the subject off your mind. Are you OK?" said Kay to Maria, placing a hand on her arm.

Too shocked to shed a tear, Maria felt the despair ooze from her eyes, which slid from Fiona and Kay to the table where the pretty, blonde girl and her ex-boyfriend sat.

"I'm OK," she hoarsely replied, remembering that only a few weeks ago, Mike had proposed and their happy engagement was planned.

The waitress appeared, serving the housemates their meals before dashing away.

"I wonder how we split," Maria sorely thought, picking up her fork and aimlessly stabbing her lunch. "It must have been over something big - for him to give me the look that he did as he came in the door."

Within minutes, Fiona and Kay had devoured their meals, Maria having struggled to eat only half of her own; and as no one craved a dessert, Kay asked for the bill; while Mike and his girlfriend rose from their seats before leaving the café in haste as Maria looked on.

"Do you want to go home after this?" Fiona said to Maria, noticing the hurt in her eyes, as the waitress returned and presented the bill.

"Yes - that's if neither of you mind," said Maria with a sigh, finding it hard to accept the harsh fact that Mike had turned cold.

"Not to worry, Maria," Kay kindly replied, as she and Fiona promptly settled the bill. "We'll drop you back home before we go on. It's probably best that you're given some space after seeing your ex with that girl."

"Have either of you seen her before?" Maria enquired, as the three women rose from their seats and put on their coats.

"*Kay* hasn't," Fiona replied as they made for the door, "But *I've* come across her - only very briefly - when she came to the door with a pen Mike had left behind on the desk where he worked. She said her name was Polly, and that she'd recently transferred to the office next to his. She didn't know his address at the time - but had seen him turn up at ours. She was no better than a stalker - that Polly; I could tell she had her eye on him as soon as she appeared on the scene," she critically went on, as the housemates exited the café and headed for the car.

Maria bit her lip as they got in the car, staying silent all the way home, until wishing her housemates a pleasant afternoon before they set off. Rivers of tears flowed down her cheeks as she stumbled upstairs to her room, studying her dead idol's poster whilst checking her purse to find it void of all cash except for one meagre pound coin.

Discarding her shoes, she lay down on the bed, a number of unanswered questions bombarding her mind as her pillow grew wet: "How and when did my pop idol die? How and why did I become unemployed? Why did Mike and I split? Did he dump *me*, or did I catch him with Polly - the girl he was with in the café - and decide to not see him again? Why are my housemates no longer the same - and how come they knew *me* when I didn't know *them*?"

Then the questions died out, superseded by an enigmatic vacuum Maria could not see, but very strongly felt - sucking her forwards in a circular gust - like a Catherine wheel visible to ghosts but not to those of the harsh, material world.

"What's happening?" Maria called out, as the strength of the vacuum increased. "Haven't I been through enough for today?"

"But this *isn't* today," she heard a voice wail in a cold, mocking tone as she opened her eyes, seeing by the clock near her bed that morning had arrived.

She pulled herself up from the bed to glance at the wall: the poster had gone; and once having slipped on her shoes, she observed that the shape of her room was oblong once more. Realising Mike would be up at this time, she switched on her phone, dialling his number to check if they were still friends.

"Oh, Mike!" she breathlessly cried as he answered the call, "I've just had this terrible dream. I dreamt that Ray Silverton was dead, that I'd lost my job, and that we had split up and you were seeing someone else. Is the concert this evening still on?"

"*Of course* the concert's still on," assured Mike, "— and Ray Silverton's very much alive. Oh - and by the way," he added, amid radio blasts from the other end of the line, "I bought my new suit for the office yesterday; it was just what I hoped I would find."

"And what about the outfit for tonight?" Maria enquired, finding it odd that he had placed more importance on new clothes for work.

"Oh, I never got round to doing that; not enough time," he casually replied. One of my colleagues is leaving next week, and we're going for drinks after work - so I'd better look smart."

"I hope the new colleague turns out to be OK," Maria remarked, aware of how two-faced the office environment could be.

"I've already met her; she's very nice. We were both introduced the other day. She's very young - still only in her teens. Anyway, Maria – got to go now. See you at a quarter past two," Mike hastily replied, before Maria, (remembering Polly – the girl who had replaced her in her dream), could ask him her name.

Assuring herself her suspicions had merely been based on the unpleasant dream, Maria abandoned the bed, freshening up in the sink before going downstairs. Edging open the kitchen door, she sighed with relief when she saw Ann and Lara chatting away, instantly turning their heads as she entered the room.

"Good morning, Maria; did you have a nice sleep?" Ann asked in her usual, positive tone; her hand covering an item of flat, glossy paper that lay by her plate.

"Not really," Maria replied, recalling her dream, "— and good morning to you both, by the way."

"Morning, Maria. You look tired; couldn't you sleep?" Lara piped up, sipping her mug of hot tea.

"I *could* - but I had a bad dream in which I was sharing a house with two housemates I didn't even know," Maria replied.

Lara and Ann exchanged looks, as Maria sat down, clasping the mug of hot tea that Lara had poured.

"Actually, Maria, we've some news to announce," confirmed Ann, as she held up the flat, glossy item that revealed the image of a large, detached house with an arched front door for Maria to see. "Lara and I are moving out in a few weeks' time - when two new tenants are due to move in. I'll be moving in with Jake; this is where he lives," she added, pointing to the image in her grasp.

"That was rather sudden; I never knew you'd plans to move out," said Maria, caught unawares.

Lara and Ann exchanged glances again, the latter lowering her eyes before speaking once more.

"Well, you're going to know, anyway, what I'm about to tell you next - as soon as you receive your copy of the circular letter from the kitchen headquarters at work - so I may as well tell you in advance," Ann reticently said, pausing before going on. "Our kitchen is closing this summer; we're losing our jobs - and I won't be able to carry on paying my share of the rent. I heard the bad news from Kim; she received her letter last week."

"And Lara - what about *you*? Why are *you* moving out?" Maria asked, feeling as if her whole world were about to cave in.

"I've found a flat of my own," Lara gladly announced, triumphantly stretching her arms in the air as she spoke. "It was the first flat I viewed - and I fell in love with it straight away. I didn't want to tell you before now, in case it fell through."

"Oh, I see; congratulations," Maria half-heartedly

replied, hoping that Mike would take a leaf from Jake's book and support her once she was jobless and poor.

"Who's that at the door at such an untimely hour?" Ann curiously asked, as the doorbell loudly rang out.

"I'll go and see," said Maria, hurrying out of the kitchen and into the hall, before freeing the chain from the latch.

"Hello. I'm a new colleague of Mike's. I was just passing this way, and wondered if he was around," said a pretty, blonde girl of maybe nineteen, as Maria pulled open the door.

"He's not here right now; can I pass a message on?" Maria tersely replied, thinking it odd that this girl had come a long way to speak to a person that she hardly knew.

Maria watched in dismay as the girl took out a sleek, silver pen from her bag. It was a pen that Mike often used - a birthday gift that had cost Maria the earth.

"Mike left this behind on his desk. I could have waited until Monday to give it to him - but thought I'd drop it in on my way," said the vivacious blonde, handing Maria the pen with an artificial smile.

"This is not where Mike lives," Maria heard herself snap, "but thanks, anyway, for your time. I'll give him the pen when I see him later on. Who shall I say dropped it in?"

"Tell him Polly called," the girl perkily said; her pretty, green eyes lighting up.

"Have a nice day," Maria said, cutting the conversation short, whereupon Polly bid her goodbye before turning away.

Maria slammed the front door and marched down the hall, appalled that last night's ill dream was coming to pass.

"Who was that?" Lara asked, as she entered the room looking glum.

"No one we know - just a girl asking directions who'd lost her way," Maria vaguely replied, reluctant to talk about the girl she had met - the girl who was about to take her boyfriend away.

"Don't be sad," Lara said to Maria, seeing the low look on her face, and gently sitting her down in the chair by her own. "You'll find another job soon - and me, you and Ann can still all see each other on a night out," she consolingly added, sensing Maria may have felt she and Ann had let her down by planning to move out.

Without uttering a word, Maria slowly nodded and lowered her eyes, already feeling that Lara and Ann were locked in the past and that she was now wholly alone.

Ann glanced at her watch.

"Lara - look at the time!" she exclaimed, hastily clearing the table of cutlery and plates. "The new tenants should be round to meet Maria and discuss a few things. They told us they'd be here between now and one o' clock - and could arrive at any minute now."

"Why wasn't *I* told?" Maria thought, throwing her housemates a glance of tacit reproof.

"Talk of the devil; looks like they're here!" Lara said as the doorbell rang out.

"I'll get it," said Ann, shooting out of the kitchen and into the hall to answer the door.

In an instant, Ann reappeared; the two future tenants left out in the hall, waiting for her to invite them into the lounge.

"Now, Maria, let me introduce you to your new housemates," said Ann.

Ann opened the door and revealed the two faces behind; Maria's blood running cold as she saw who they were.

"Hello, Maria," the new housemates greeted in turn, as Maria found herself staring in shock at the blonde and the girl with red hair she had met in the dream which had pushed her life forward by months, presenting a disquieting foretaste of what was to come.

SUNSHINE AND MASKS

"Stay safe; stay well; keep washing your hands," the disc jockey said at the end of his shift as the news was about to be aired; and as the newscaster announced further deaths from the vicious pandemic infecting the world, Liz switched the radio off, loath to hear more as she put on her coat, pushing her fear of going outside to the back of her mind.

"Those online supermarket sites are a pain. There are no delivery slots till the beginning of June - and I'll starve if I wait until then," she frustratingly thought, fetching her purse which she placed in her carrier bag.

Liz took a deep breath and made for the door - her dread of catching the virus through contact with cash, a carton or a can, or from drawing too close to another human being in the supermarket aisle - sending shivers down her spine as she ventured outside, wondering how long the virus would last, and if it would recur.

The virus was known as "Covid-19"- a pandemic said to have been caused by a wet market somewhere in Wuhan - which had mutated and become worse, forcing schools, restaurants and offices to close, police to patrol the streets, and people to remain in their homes - at least until the death rate rapidly declined.

Liz should have been glad for the excuse to stay indoors and keep to herself for the very first time; she had suffered from anxiety for years - a condition rendering her 'unwilling' by managers at work, due to her fear of being allocated tasks impossible to grasp or to finish in time.

Her sister, too, had always been "the favourite" amongst aunts, uncles, teachers, neighbours, and everyone she knew; and her mother would come round - (like relatives should to 'keep the family close') - spouting remarks on how 'perfect' her sister had turned out to be as compared to herself. As for friends, Liz had few left; most of them having lost patience once having asked her to parties and frenzied nights out that would fill her with absolute dread, forcing her to turn their kind offers down.

Yes - the chance to distance herself from her fellow human beings had finally arrived. But this situation was different from before: this was an 'invisible war,' and everyone was scared. So for Liz, it was not a question of choice between living in close contact with others who made your life hell, and living on your own amongst Covid-19 - away from their jibes.

"Oi you - stand back! "Call that social distancing? If you happen to be asymptomatic, you've given me Covid-19!" yelled an angry, male voice at a female shopper passing by, disrupting Liz's thoughts as she reached the store entrance in dread

The woman straightened her mask before hurrying away, the provisions rattling in her bag as she headed for her car that was parked a few metres away.

"That shopper is scared," Liz thought, as she picked up a basket and entered the grocery store. "That's why he let rip at that woman; his fear was aggression in disguise."

Putting on her gloves before cleaning the handles of her basket with wipes provided by the store, Liz got out the list of provisions she hoped would be at hand to buy, peering down the aisles at all the shoppers wearing masks, ignoring warnings from circular markers on the supermarket floor to keep two metres apart.

Venturing further down the aisle, she found the first item on her list missing from the shelf; but how could she approach the assistant pricing goods, and ask if more milk had been stocked in the storeroom downstairs? Settling for milk of a skimmed, powdered kind and a few more items on the list that she was able to find, Liz joined the supermarket queue, standing two metres apart from the customer in front, to be served five minutes later by a masked shop assistant wearing gloves, ensconced behind a large, protective screen.

Reluctant to stay out for too long, Liz hurried back home, sighing as she studied the items on her list, half of which still needed to be bought.

"No supermarket delivery slots, and nothing on the shelves," she murmured to herself as she switched the radio on and stored her provisions away.

Waves of anxiety pummelled her gut, transmitting through the rest of her body, as the newscaster announced that the number of deaths overnight had increased to three hundred and four. The previous day, the figure had dropped from three hundred and one to two hundred and ten - a sign that the virus was not on the wane as the Government claimed. Moreover, a vaccine to make one immune to the virus had yet to be found, and people would soon be forced back to work because of the threat of a global depression resulting from Covid-19 having kept them indoors.

Liz drew another deep breath: how long was this wretched pandemic going to pursue? How many more would it kill - and would she, her mother and sister come out of it alive? More terrifying questions invaded her head, until after one long, anxious gasp, she pulled out the plug and the radio went dead, as the menacing wail of an ambulance started outside.

It was a quarter past two, and her unopened post had been lying in the lobby downstairs for over three hours. Having waited for any germs to die down, Liz put on her gloves, looking alert when descending the stairs in case anyone happening to be passing her way drew too close.

Relieved that the lobby was empty, she dug through the post, hurrying back to her flat with a parcel and letter in her grasp. Studying the envelope of the letter more closely, she saw it was sent by the place where she worked; from where she had been on leave for the past several weeks - just before the virus had peaked and lockdown was enforced. She was on furlough pay that covered eighty per cent of what she usually earned before Covid-19 - when staff could liaise as a 'loyal' and 'harmonious' team.

Seating herself at the table in the kitchen with a cup of hot tea, Liz opened the envelope in dread, the letter inside it confirming her fears that her furlough had ceased. She emitted an instinctive sigh, scared of returning to work, as the virus had not gone away. She did not own a cycle, and lived too far away from work to commute there on foot. Scores of bus and tube drivers had sadly succumbed to Covid-19 - and how could passengers keep two metres apart when having to scramble on board, either to stand on a packed train or bus, or sit on a seat near another to save precious space?

Placing the wretched letter aside, she picked up the parcel with dread, having realized her mother had sent it minutes ago when seeing it lying amongst the litter of post in the lobby downstairs. Peeling off the strip of tape that had kept it intact, Liz pulled out the contents inside: two polythene bags - one containing disposable gloves; the other stuffed with protective, reusable masks. A note from her mother was also enclosed, which Liz had found buried beneath the contents of the bag.

Bracing herself for lectures and brutal home truths, she held in her breath, perusing the first few lines of the note with alarm.

"Dear Liz,"

the letter began,

> *"I hope you're remembering to wear gloves while collecting your post - as well as wearing your mask while going to the shops. As you can see, I've sent you another supply in case you run out. And please - if anyone asks to come round, put them off; and if they turn up at your door, don't let them in.*
>
> *I heard on the news that another three hundred and four people died of the virus last night; it looks as if this awful pandemic will never go away - and being an asthmatic, I doubt if I'll survive a second wave---."*

Liz swallowed a few sips of tea, which began to grow cold, reflecting on her mother's miserable, pessimistic words: did the woman not realize that her daughter was depressed - even at the easiest of times? Why was she failing to take this fact into account? Liz put down her cup with a sigh; the only consolation she could find to mitigate her mother's dark words was the fact that the woman was no scientific ace, and that like the Spanish Flu of 1918 which had claimed millions of lives, Covid-19 could burn itself out in a matter of time.

Liz refolded the note, placing it aside with the letter from the firm where she worked: she had read more than enough for one gruelling day.

"I don't need this," she heard herself groan, feeling frustrated and trapped; her face forming into a frown as she delved for the mask that lay buried in her bag. Despite the pandemic, she felt that she had to get out, and leaving the rest of her tea to grow horridly cold, she quickly got up, fetching her coat before leaving the flat once again.

Meeting the air, she saw that the sun had come out, tempting too many civilians out onto the street in the midst of this sly, silent war. The supermarket she had visited less than two hours ago was far busier now; a long queue of shoppers with trolleys two metres apart, waiting to enter the store which only admitted a few desperate shoppers at any one time. Turning the corner at the end of the road, she saw no policemen about, having heard on the news that thousands of people had been fined during lockdown for breaking the rules.

Still feeling upset by the post she received, Liz stopped at the nearest bench she was able to find, which was outside the church, 3 minutes' walk from her flat. She sat down with a sigh as she tried to unwind; a mixture of thoughts going round in her head which she longed to erase. She tried to practise an exercise aired on the breakfast television show for calming the nerves; sitting back whilst closing her eyes and counting to ten - only to find on opening them again that the black thoughts returned.

"I say! My dear - are you all right?" she heard a voice cry, as she noticed an elderly lady sitting on the bench by her own - two metres away.

"Yes, thanks," Liz tensely replied, caught unawares.

The old woman slowly sat up, the tip of her grey, metal stick grasped in her hand. Her face wore a faint, kindly smile; her eyes deeply fixed on the woman who could not relax.

"Forgive me for saying so, dear," she reflectively began, continuing to stare, "but as I was taking my afternoon stroll, I spotted you sitting on the bench - and noticed you looked a bit fazed. At first I thought you were feeling unwell when I saw you closing your eyes. Do you happen to suffer with your nerves?"

Liz looked down in shame. She hated others referring to the nervous disposition with which she had been 'blessed;' and had this senior citizen not been informed that those over seventy years old should not be making a habit of going out of doors in these uncertain times?

"Yes, I do," Liz grudgingly replied, looking up at the woman while straightening her mask.

"I *thought* you did; I can see it on your face; my Brian's exactly the same - but I suppose we're *all* a bit jittery now," the woman apologetically remarked.

"Critical old bag - drawing attention to my nerves when it's none of her concern. How would she like it if I told her she wouldn't be able to walk without the aid of a stick?" Liz peevishly thought, trying to appear as polite as she possibly could.

She flashed the old woman a smile without uttering a word, feeling the urge to walk off in order to avoid more unwanted remarks.

"Hasn't it turned out to be a lovely afternoon?" the old woman said, looking up at the cloudless, blue sky.

"Yes," Liz tersely replied, not wishing to converse.

"My Brian will probably be out in the garden right now - enjoying the sun. Shame he's unable to come round. He gives me a call every week, but it isn't the same. He's such a good son - not the type to take to the beach and ignore lockdown rules on a warm, sunny day," the old lady went on, making Liz cringe.

"It's awful when you hear of people flouting the rules. After all, how do we know we're not asymptomatic, and aren't passing on Covid-19 to somebody else?" remarked Liz, softening a bit as she thought of the hoards of people who had flocked to Southend only last week, ignoring the Government's advice not to travel too far.

"Any one of us could be carriers, my dear," the other agreed, tightening the grip on her stick. "And as soon as I think a place is about to get crowded, I'm off."

The old woman paused, looking down at the ground with nostalgic, grey eyes.

"My grandmother lived through the Spanish Flu of 1918," she went on, as Liz listened with intent, keen to hear more. "At the time it first struck, she was living with her husband on a farm."

"It struck a *second* time?" the other exclaimed, unaware of this fact.

"*And* a third," the old lady confirmed, staring into the younger woman's eyes. "My grandmother must only have been twenty-one or twenty-two at the time. The first wave was generally mild - and most who'd caught it recovered - but the second was absolutely deadly; killed millions of people worldwide. More First World War troops were killed from that virus than the war. I remember my grandmother having said that in Europe and America, soldiers travelling by boat and by train brought the flu into cities and that it spread to the countryside from there."

"And what about the *third* wave?" Liz curiously enquired, her anxiety beginning to rise.

"That came in the spring of 1919," the old woman said, with a look to suggest that the world had been cursed. "It wasn't as severe as the second - and didn't last long. By the summer of that year, it was gone; but no one knew how long it would last at the time," she added with a sigh, cross that the pandemic had blighted her grandmother's life. "At the time, there were no ventilators, vaccines or anti-virals of any kind - so that hardly helped. But just like today, schools, offices, churches, restaurants, and other public places were closed; people wore masks, couldn't shake hands, and had to stay in their homes until the virus died down."

"Oh dear," uttered Liz, unnerved by the older woman's words. "I hope that *this* virus won't be as bad."

"No two pandemics are ever the same," the old woman confirmed, throwing Liz a reassuring smile. "This, my dear, is Covid-19; it's totally new. The Spanish Flu will never strike again. We can only keep our fingers crossed that Covid-19 won't be as bad."

"I wasn't ready for this," Liz remarked, angry that the virus had not gone away. "Only a few months ago, I didn't see it coming - and at the end of last year, thought 2020 would turn out to be like any other year."

"*None of us* saw it coming, my dear. Covid-19 could have struck twenty years ago, or at any other time: all it takes is for a flu virus to suddenly shift," the woman replied, causing Liz to fall silent again.

Liz dwelled on the old woman's words in relation to the anxious condition with which she was plagued. Of all the nightmares she had feared would come true, day after day - from the moment her illness came on to the evening that lockdown was enforced - the dread of a possible pandemic endangering the world had not crossed her mind. Even when Covid-19 was announced, and raged in Wuhan, she never suffered sleepless nights, scared that the virus would spread to her part of the world and fiercely take hold. And now, she was worrying for her niece - the child her sister had borne - whose life may be claimed by another pandemic sullying the Earth in twenty years' time.

"Have I frightened you, dear?" the old woman asked, staring at Liz with concern.

"*Of course* you have, you nasty, old witch. But you think I'm a nervous wreck, anyway - so what difference does it make?" Liz angrily thought, throwing the woman another false smile whilst biting her tongue.

"Try not to worry, my dear," the other advised; her sallow, lined face lighting up in the glare of the sun. "All we can do in these uncertain times is take each day as it comes - and hope for the best."

Liz rose from the bench; there was nothing this elderly lady could say to cure her of her nerves; nothing she could do to extend her furlough pay, or to help her go up in her mother's esteem. Above everything else, this woman could not turn back the clock and reverse the unhappy events of Liz's past; she could not erase the emotional baggage Liz carried today.

"Look - I have to go; there's something I must do," uttered Liz, picking up her bag from the bench, about to turn away.

"I do hope I haven't disturbed you, my dear," the old woman said, noticing how fraught Liz appeared.

"It's my niece's birthday at the end of the week; I must send her some money and a card," the younger woman stammered, avoiding a direct reply, as the woman remained sitting on the bench, squinting in the sun's potent rays. "Bye, then," Liz added, hurrying away.

"Bye, my dear! Hope you manage to send off your niece's card and money in time!" the old woman called out, as Liz crossed the road, submerging round the corner of the street towards the safety of her flat.

She stopped off at the small corner shop to purchase the card, halting when reaching the entrance to put on her gloves, check that her mask was still straight, and peer through the door to make sure there was no one inside.

Seconds later, she entered the shop, making her way down the aisle to view the selection of cards on display at the back, choosing the one with the glittery horse which she bought with contaminated cash. Seeing another shopper about to come in, Liz exited the shop, slipping the greetings card into her bag as she made her way home. Not knowing how to send the money online, she would send it by post in pristine cash notes, which she would advise her niece not to touch until after the first few hours of opening the card, in order to allow any germs they may carry to die down. She was already regarded as the "family black sheep" by everybody else, and did not wish to make her reputation worse by being known as the "poisonous aunt."

Re-entering her flat and removing her coat, she entered the lounge, fetching the handful of ten pound notes which she placed in the card. She penned a few lines of good wishes before sealing the flap of the envelope down and leaving it aside, telling herself she would post it tomorrow when everything was 'quiet.'

She decided to catch up on the channel now airing the breakfast program shown several hours ago, and switched the set on to the slot that announced the various workers whose lives had been claimed by Covid-19 overnight. These were all 'hero' key workers on the 'front line:' a hospital doctor from Walton-on-Thames; a carer and mother of three who had worked in an old people's home; a male nurse who had been in the country for only ten months, and a supermarket cashier of only nineteen were among the list to fall ill and die saving other people's lives.

Tears welled up in Liz's eyes, which struggled to stay on the screen, absorbing image after image of the heroes that were lost - until they found they could take it no more, urging Liz's instincts to rise from the couch and turn off the set. Returning to the couch, Liz cowered in shame - mixed with a feeling of guilt, as she loathed her 'waste of space' self for lacking the courage these heroes possessed, without wishing she were one of them at the same time.

And now, everything was quiet; no news about Covid-19 bruising her ears. Her eyes slid towards the envelope lying on the table, waiting to be sent; its flap transmitting an invisible smile to the woman a stone's throw away. Liz got out a pen from her bag and a stamp from her purse, picking up the envelope on which she began writing her niece's address; the news about Covid-19 returning to haunt.

She put her pen down in the silence of the flat; her mind asking fate questions; working overtime.

"When will the pandemic die out?"

"Will a second wave occur - and if it does, when will it strike—?"

A TRIP TO WORLD'S END

It was nearly midday, and the chambermaid arrived, ready to clean up the rooms. Gemma threw the domestic a glance as she made for the lift, stepping hurriedly inside as it promptly arrived. Whilst pressing the button labelled 'G,' she found herself standing near a middle-aged man in a grey suit and tie who looked frustrated and cross; his mobile telephone gripped tightly to his ear.

"I want my money back - NOW!" he yelled in a strident, American drawl that grated her nerves. "Call yourself a cab firm? My senile aunt could have done a better job; even *she'd* have more of an idea of knowing where to go. I wouldn't even recommend you to anyone for free!"

Gemma eyed the man with unease; his large, chubby face turning crimson with rage; his brash, strident voice growing more and more loud as he sighed and continued to rant.

"Whatever happened to 'the customer always being right?' I asked to be taken to 'The British Museum' - not on a detour to some damnable hole on the cab driver's whim---!"

Gemma could not believe what she heard; why would a cab driver take a customer to somewhere he did not want to go?

As the lift stopped at the ground floor, the doors slid apart, allowing its two passengers out; the exasperated man stomping off towards the lounge, continuing to bruise the cab controller's ears, as Gemma headed for the foyer, fumbling through her bag for the key to the room she had hired.

"Is there another park around here? I've already seen Green Park and St James's Square," she said to the woman at the desk as she handed in her key.

"Apart from Green Park and St James's Square, the nearest park is 'Soho Square.' It's a few kilometres from here, and is quite a long walk. If you're tired, you could hire a cab, or jump on a bus," the receptionist advised, eyeing her guest through the glasses that slid down her nose.

Gemma spent a few seconds deciding on what she should do. Walking to 'Soho Square' would make her trip free, which would mean extra cash for a more enjoyable lunch.

"Would you like me to order you a cab from the hotel?" the receptionist asked, aware that Gemma was struggling to make up her mind.

"No thanks - I'll walk," Gemma said, unsure of the route to the square, but prioritising lunch.

"OK then, Madam - have a nice day," the receptionist said.

"Thanks," the other replied, before turning away, and hoping she would not get lost.

Gemma exited the hotel, already shrinking in her vision as she passed the candy floss stall that stood metres away. Turning the corner into a street of museums and shops, she noticed a map of the area surrounding the hotel displayed in a telephone booth which she stopped to peruse, to discover she was in Piccadilly - an area which she had not visited before.

Reaching a side road with places to eat, her hunger began to increase, and no longer being able to hold out, she plumped for the quaint-looking café on her right near a kiosk selling ice cream.

Peering through the glass-fronted door, she saw that the café was full - but aware that time was getting on, and soon lunchtime would end, she ambled inside, hoping a table at which she could sit would shortly be free. Joining the queue of customers waiting to be served, she heard the two women in front discussing the gossip of the town.

"Did you hear about the cab firm said to be somewhere in West London not taking its customers to where they've been asking to go?" said one to the other, taking Gemma's mind back to the man with the phone in the lift.

"No. Whoever told you that?" the other exclaimed as they neared the front of the queue.

"A couple were telling me about it in the lounge - yesterday evening, after you retired to your room with a headache for a quiet, early night," answered the first.

"Not *all* rumours are true," said the other, frowning in doubt. "I bet that couple hadn't suffered that experience themselves," she added with a snort.

"No - but they claimed they met someone who *had*; it was a person on the coach who stayed in another hotel around here," said the first, getting ready to be served.

"Did they mention the name of the cab firm involved?" asked the second, still unconvinced.

"'West London Cars,' I think they were called; but they told me the cab was hailed - not booked in advance - and that, apparently, the person who hailed it never saw a name displayed on the car," said the first, eagerly eyeing the emptying seats at the table nearby.

"Not all cabs have their name on the front," the second sceptically replied, still convinced that the rumours related by the couple were false.

"Well, what *I've* heard has put me right off," retorted the first, somewhat annoyed that her words were being dismissed. "And the next time we leave the hotel for an 'Oxford Street' shop and feel too tired to walk back, you can chance a trip back in a cab by yourself; I'll take a bus!" she crossly went on, silencing her friend as they paid for their meals and made for the table with the seats still yet to be filled.

Gemma took out her purse, looking behind her for another available seat on which she could sit after ordering her meal. She peered, once again, at the menu on the wall, still trying to decide whether to opt for the vegetable lasagne or chicken en croute, amid sighs of impatience from those standing behind.

"Can I help you? What do you want?" the male barista sullenly barked; his manner suggesting that Gemma was stalling the queue.

"Please could I have the vegetable lasagne?" Gemma asked, almost dropping her purse with unease.

"We haven't any left; is there anything else you would like?" the barista said.

"The chicken en croute?" Gemma hesitantly asked, realising the café was full and that some of its food had run out.

"*That's* all gone, too," the assistant replied; the rest of the queue restlessly sighing again.

"Then could I have the macaroni cheese with courgettes - and buttered bread on the side?" Gemma asked, her stomach aching through not having eaten since supper the previous day.

The assistant emitted a sigh, and threw her a critical glance.

"Drink?" he impatiently asked, vexed that she had not asked him before. Gemma studied the menu again.

"Could I have a soda and lime?" she asked, cowed by the man's icy glare.

She fought the urge to storm out of the café in a huff, as the man took the money for her meal before passing her a bottle of soda and lime from the medley of drinks at his side. With her drink in her hand, she abandoned the queue, sidling down the aisle of the café in search of a seat. She gunned for the table near the door on spotting two tourists vacating their seats, only to be beaten to the chase by a couple with a boisterous child. But the next few moments brought Gemma more luck, when a family of six settled their bill and made their exit at once, leaving her with a table all to herself.

As she sat, waiting to be served, the intolerance aimed at her by the assistant and those in the long, hungry queue re-entered her mind; but this had not been the first time. Others often reacted towards her like this; and she sighed in regret, reflecting on never having been the popular type, despite meaning well. Although unsure of why others treated her in this contemptuous way, she suspected the anxious condition with which she was plagued from the age of thirteen played a key part - and felt she would win more respect had it never emerged. This was why she preferred to go out on her own; feeling uneasy and misunderstood when attempting to mix. Yet as a child, Gemma had felt happy and not overwhelmed; her outlook was hopeful and bold, and her trust in others made her a distant cry from the cowed, wary soul into which she had gradually turned.

A waitress approached with her meal, rupturing her thoughts; the golden glaze of the macaroni cheese and the verdant courgettes dampened her ravenous mouth, reminding her of how hungry she had felt since leaving the hotel.

Minutes later she was back in "Golden Square" without knowing where she was, looking up her dog-eared A-Z before entering another alien street inhabited by shops. She eyed the shop on her right - a huge department store on four floors selling clothes, accessories and shoes. Gemma looked away with a yawn; she had too many clothes as it was - all the more so since she hardly went out, and did not need to look smart in the job that she held.

She noticed a jewellers ahead, and remembering the silver drop earring she lost on the street and needed to replace, decided to walk on until reaching the little glass window she wished to look through. She eyed the selection of earrings neatly on show, looking for a pair similarly designed to the one she had lost - only to sigh in despair when she came across nothing that matched. Pushing open the door, she entered the shop, hoping to find different sorts of earrings inside.

"Can I help you?" the shop assistant asked as he saw her appear.

"Do you sell any earrings like these?" she enquired, showing him the earring that matched the one she had lost.

"I'm afraid they're no longer in fashion, so aren't in demand," the assistant replied. "You must have got them a long time ago; we haven't been selling that style of earring for years."

Gemma lowered her eyes, returning the earring to her bag.

"Yes, I did; they were a present from my father - forty years ago - not long before he died," she sadly replied.

The assistant threw her a glance to suggest that she should have moved on, and ceased mourning the death of her father a long time ago.

"Is there anything else here that catches your eye? We have plenty of beautiful up-to-date earrings on show," he heedlessly asked, pointing to the earrings lying in the cabinet of glass by his side.

"No thanks. Have a nice day," Gemma snapped, taking offence that her grief had been cruelly dismissed.

Flouncing out of the shop, she went on her way,

continuing to walk until she calmed down and her feet started to ache. She decided to rest on the bench positioned on her right; but taking a seat, she felt tense, and knew something was wrong. She felt irreversibly damaged; traumatised, in a strange kind of way. It was hard for a person to gauge the position in which they were awkwardly trapped; and those on the outside looking in never cared to point out what they saw.

"What's wrong with me?" she thought with a feeling of shame. "Why haven't I lived a full life, like everyone else - such as marry, bear children, and have lots of friends? Did my past do me damage, or am I less normal than I thought?" But it was no use; no definite answer would come; simply the usual 'ifs' and 'maybes' still entering her mind.

Gemma glanced at her watch. It was nearly two o' clock, and she needed to reach "Soho Square" as soon as she could to avoid missing out on dinner at the hotel. She abandoned the bench, looking about her to find herself totally lost; not knowing what bus to jump on, or which tube train to take.

She crossed the road and turned a corner to reach the next street, hoping that she would catch up with the stranger ahead.

"Me not know 'Soho Square.' Me tourist," the stranger casually shrugged, after she managed to reach him and ask him if he knew the way.

"Oh, I see," she replied in despair, wondering who else she could ask as he scurried away.

Seconds later, a bright yellow cab pulled up on the kerb; the driver's head popping out of its door as the window wound down.

"Are you lost?" he asked, seeing her frantically pull out her map from her bag.

"Unfortunately, I *am*," Gemma said with a sigh. "I'd wanted to get to 'Soho Square;' do you know the way?"

The cab driver grinned, revealing a row of gold teeth that dazzled her eyes.

"It's only a stone's throw from here," he replied. "Have you been to West London before?"

"Only ever once - a few decades ago," she confirmed, checking her watch once again. "I come from the Isle of Wight, and don't usually travel this far."

"Finding your way around is hard when you don't know the roads," the driver remarked, pinning his eyes on the A-Z in her grasp. "I could get you to 'Soho Square' in no time at all; do you want to jump in?" he went on, clicking open the door near the rear of cab.

Without further thought, Gemma clamoured onboard, securing her belt before placing the map in her bag.

"Glad to see you're strapped up," the driver remarked, as he started the cab which he got into gear, before turning a corner and leaving the pavement behind.

"Where are we now?" Gemma asked as they reached a main road with restaurants and shops, bustling with tourists and buskers performing for cash.

"Oxford Street," the driver replied, switching the radio on as they passed a green light.

A few minutes later, she glanced at her watch, and remembering the driver having said 'Soho Square' would be moments away, wondered why she still sat at the back of the cab.

"How much further is it *now*?" she called out.

But the driver did not reply, the blare from his radio making more noise as the cab picked up speed.

"Why is this taking so long?" Gemma asked, trying to make her voice heard as the music blared out.

The cab sped past Marble Arch, entering 'Bayswater Road' which looked onto Hyde Park.

"I've seen a photo of 'Soho Square' - and this isn't it," Gemma cried, sensing the cab had been heading the incorrect way; but the driver drove heedlessly on as if he were deaf.

"Stop the cab now! I want to get out!" Gemma yelled; but the driver still did not speak, steering her even further into the unknown.

"I've been in here too long, and haven't enough money to cover the fare!" she desperately cried, afraid that the driver was planning something adverse.

Once half an hour had passed, the car stopped at a close; and it was then that the radio went dead as the cab driver switched off the engine and blandly looked round.

"Oh no - I'm going to be raped!" Gemma thought, frozen with fear as the driver studied her closely with predatory eyes. The chauffeur, however, looked away, sitting back as he unclipped his seat belt and tossed it aside.

Gemma cowered in the back of the cab, as a man in a suit and white shoes emerged from a crack in the cul-de-sac blocking the street. She wondered what would come next as the man drew nearer to the cab, halting when reaching the bright yellow driver's side door.

The driver wound down the pane, poking his head through the door to speak to the man. Gemma took a deep breath, the fear of a serious assault re-entering her mind. Not daring to utter a word, she gripped her seat belt in fright, as the driver signalled to the man in the suit with a nod.

"And now you can undo your belt and jump out of the car," the cab driver said, clicking open the doors, before climbing out.

Gemma quietly obeyed, cautiously eyeing the men as she wondered where she was. The dead end street smelt musty and surreal, emitting the aura of a past, forgotten land without a name.

"But how will I get back to the hotel? I don't know

where I am!" she heard herself ask, eyeing her surroundings in despair.

"Who said anything about getting back?" asked the man in the suit.

"But I *need* to get back," Gemma said, eyeing her watch. "It's getting late - and I don't want to miss my dinner at the hotel."

The men exchanged looks and then laughed; the driver heedlessly locking the doors of the cab causing Gemma to flinch.

"You needn't be afraid. Dinner can wait; there's a higher priority right now. Come with us, and we'll show you what it is," said the man in the suit, he and the driver walking over to her side

As frightened as Gemma had felt about what the two men may have planned, she followed them in silence as they made for the cul-de-sac ahead, which housed an alley in its core into which they walked until they reached the other end.

"Keep going," said the man in the suit as they emerged into another dead end street that looked onto a harbour of boats; her legs feeling limp and like jelly; struggling to walk.

The men stopped at a single-storey building made of red bricks, casually letting themselves and Gemma inside. She followed them into a room filled with seats and a stage with a curtain at its fore, taking a seat at the front, while the men sat behind.

"Now you can watch - and ask a few questions, if you like," said the man in the suit as the curtain was raised, revealing the shadow of a man ensconced on a chair.

Gemma watched as the shadow came to life, cupping its hands and shifting its head to face the audience in front.

"Where am I?" she asked as she saw the dark figure stir.

"World's End," it replied, falling silent again, as the driver and man in the suit mutely looked on.

"Who are you?" Gemma irritably asked, her confusion mounting up. "Why aren't you showing me your face?"

"It doesn't matter who I am; no one's ever seen my face. I'm here to help you - and that's all that counts," the silhouetted man calmly said.

"Help me over *what*?" Gemma curiously asked, still scared that she might end up a victim of harm.

"Over where you've been standing all these years, and the difficulties you've had," answered the man.

"I don't understand; what do you mean?" Gemma asked.

The silhouetted man uncupped his hands, resting both palms on his knees, Gemma feeling afraid of what he would say. The man cleared his throat, letting a few seconds pass before speaking again.

"Life seems to have proved quite a struggle for you, hasn't it, Gemma? It's been an arduous struggle throughout."

As much as Gemma agreed with what the man said, she stayed quiet. His observation had hurt, making her feel she was taking the blame for something that was not her fault.

"You've struggled at school and throughout your career - and you have failed to be understood by your fellow human beings," the silhouetted man continued after a pause. "You've felt uneasy in the company of others - which has rendered you friendless, childless and a spinster as a result. As a teenager, neighbours would come round to your mother's house and berate you for being 'anti-social' and 'into yourself.' You've lost countless jobs for not networking or talking enough - and you've found it hard to multi-task. While you were at school, teachers and pupils alike were unkind and gave you a hard time; and you'd often come home wondering what you'd done wrong. Oh dear, Gemma - you haven't been very popular, have you?"

The shadow's blunt words cut Gemma like a knife; they were all the more painful because they were true. She longed to ask him how he knew about the problems she had faced, but her tongue and lips froze.

"Do you recognise the hardships that I've just pointed out?" the man asked, cupping his hands once again.

"Yes," Gemma said, lowering her eyes with regret and a feeling of shame.

"You need not feel guilty; none of it has ever been your fault - even though you've carried all the blame," acknowledged the man, providing Gemma with a feeling of relief and the need to hear more.

"Yes, Gemma - that's right - you haven't been to blame for the problems you've faced; and there's a reason for this - a reason beyond your control. In your long-term struggle with relationships, work and time spent at school, you've felt frustrated and confused through not knowing why these struggles have occurred," the silhouetted man resumed with a hint of resignation in his tome. "You cannot be cured; but self-realisation is the key to easing your discontent."

"Am I mentally ill?" Gemma asked, aware that her anxious condition was far more than mild.

"No," the man flatly replied, "but you have a disorder, nonetheless. Surely there must have been times when you've sat down alone and have wondered what was wrong?"

"Yes," Gemma confirmed, unable to deny that the silhouetted man was correct. "But I've never been sure of what exactly it was: what disorder do I have?"

41

"A disorder that was never diagnosed," answered the man.

Gemma's first reaction was one of dismay, followed by one of reproach; had this man's words been flames, she would now have been bearing third degree burns.

"Exactly what disorder do I have - and why was it never checked out?" she indignantly cried, outraged at what he had said.

"You suffer from Asperger's Syndrome - a developmental disorder characterised by significant difficulties in social interactive and non-verbal communication," confirmed the silhouetted man. "The disorder is only very mild, but it's hampered your life nonetheless. As for why your family never had you diagnosed is hardly a question for me. Your family and I have never met, so I can't tell you why. But it's said that quite often, parents are in denial - and would rather turn a blind eye to the problems their own offspring face than admit a disorder is linked to their own flesh and blood."

"I see," Gemma said, her anger dying down. "And this is why there have been so many misunderstandings between others and myself - why I've been bullied at school and lost job after job, and why I hadn't been the favoured child?"

"Unfortunately, yes," said the man on the stage, "but although there's no cure and your problems with others won't cease, you'll depart from World's End today feeling far more at peace."

"Who are you?" Gemma anxiously asked, beginning to feel better already, despite having found the reality painful to hear.

"It doesn't matter who I am," the man said. "I'm sorry to have been blunt about your condition - but I felt you had a right to be aware of it long before now."

"I suppose I should thank you. At least now I know

where I stand after all these years," Gemma said with regret.

"And now I must go," the faceless man said. "Have a safe journey back to the hotel."

The man could no longer be seen as the curtain drew down, the driver and man in the suit abandoning their seats, prompting Gemma to rise from her own.

"And now you can return to the place from where you came; the chauffeur will bring you back," said the man in the suit to Gemma, as they all exited the building and made their way back to the cab.

"Jump in," the cab driver said, clicking open the doors. "Would you like me to take you to 'Soho Square,' or straight back to the hotel?"

Gemma glanced at her watch as she got in the back of the cab; the man in the suit and the driver climbing in front.

"It's getting late," she replied, keen not to miss out on dinner at the hotel, "Please take me to 'Orchard Hotel,' Cleveland Place, SW1."

We'll get you back there in no time at all; make sure you're strapped up," said the driver, who flashed his row of gold teeth as he started the cab, releasing the handbrake in order to leave the streets of World's End far behind.

This time the driver had proved as good as his word, as in a matter of minutes, the cab had pulled up outside "Orchard Hotel."

"This was a longer journey than I'd planned; how much do I owe?" Gemma asked, unfastening her belt.

"Leave your purse where it is; the fare is on me! You take care now!" the cab driver roared as she opened the door.

"Thanks a lot - and goodbye," Gemma said before climbing out of the cab and turning away.

"Just a minute! I've something that you may have lost!" called the man in the suit, rushing out of the cab.

Gemma quickly turned back as the man sped over to her side; she saw that something was clasped in the palm of his hand.

"When I arrived at World's End this afternoon, I found this lying on the road; does it happen to be yours?" he hurriedly enquired.

Gemma's eyes stung as he opened his hand, revealing a silver drop earring resembling the one she had lost years ago - an invaluable gift from the father she could not get back. Then, as she thanked the man in the suit and took it from his hand, a memory of when she was twelve suddenly came back; it was the memory of an area near a river; an area with red brick buildings and dead end streets, where she and her father had spent the day together months before he died.

"Are you all right?" asked a porter as she entered the hotel; her face streaming with hot, nostalgic tears.

"Yes," she replied, before collecting her key from the desk. "I've been back to the place from where I came."

The porter and tourists nearby eyed her and frowned, swapping mutual looks to suggest that they thought she was strange; but this time, Gemma went calmly upstairs without wondering why, or feeling ashamed and confused.

Reaching her room, she let herself in, feeling tired as she took a seat on the dressing table chair, wondering if her encounter with the men in the cab and the silhouetted man enlightening her on a disorder she never knew she had was merely a dream.

Then Gemma opened her bag, to find the lost earring returned by the man in the suit still housed in her purse, re-united with the matching one she had kept all these years.

"The trip to World's End *was* real - so what the

44

silhouetted man had said must all have been true," she uttered to herself, as she wiped her face dry.

Gemma realised her Asperger's Syndrome would never be cured and that her difficulty with others would always remain; but all her questions were answered, now her condition was diagnosed. The chauffeur had taken her back to the place where she and her father had spent their last outing decades ago - before all the problems she miserably faced had grown worse. But today she had returned to World's End - the place from where she had come - and now felt at peace.

THE OTHER SIDE OF A WISH

Alice advanced towards the beach, and luckily no one was about; not a sound except for the lapping of the tide against the white, sandy shore. Alice had to get out and be alone for some peace, for remaining indoors would have robbed her of her mind.

Seconds later, she reached "Dryad's Cave" - a landmark of history and myths, and a magnet to tourists worldwide. Alice had visited this cave many times; it was situated minutes from her home - so to her it was just another cave - although she had never discovered the genie and the little silver lamp said to have once been discovered in the depths of its core.

But as doubtful as she was about the legends attached to "Dryad's Cave," she saw it as an object of retreat - a haven of tunnelled, limestone walls under which she could hide when life became too much to bear.

Struggling up the artificial steps, Alice wondered how long she could spend time on her own before being searched for and found; for she had cerebral palsy, and was classed as one with 'special needs,' leaving her robbed of the independence she so desperately craved.

With the maximum of effort, she reached the last step, fighting her way through the mouth of the cave and into the dark, rocky tunnel that led to its core. Minutes later, she reached her usual niche - a sizeable hollow with a section of chairs on which tourists could rest during tours.

As a very young child, Alice would visit this spot in search of the lamp, believing the myth that the genie's existence was real. There were so many wishes she wanted to make, which now as an adult, she realised no one could grant.

She sat down on a chair, rubbing her overstretched legs as she tried to unwind; the long, heated row with her family an hour ago still haunting her mind. Why had her parents allowed her sister more freedom - just because she could easily walk? Those with cerebral palsy craved freedom and pleasure like everyone else - so why were her parents so blind to the fact she felt trapped?

Sitting back in the chair with closed eyes and counting to ten, she heard something drop - a sharp, metallic sound that echoed through the hollows of the cave. She opened her eyes to discover an object at her feet; Moorish and silvery grey in the cave's meagre light. She picked up the object and studied it closely to let out a squeak of surprise when seeing a small, silver lamp - just like the one described in the myth - in the grip of her hand.

"A tourist must have placed this lamp here just to poke fun," Alice thought, sceptically rubbing the object to prove herself right.

Her hand fell still as a sudden force of heat emitted from the lamp which began to vibrate, transmitting powerful waves through the walls of the cave. Alice started in fright as it slipped from her grasp, landing at her feet as a serpent of gaseous vapour streamed from its sprout. She gasped in surprise as the steam formed into a cloud, increasing in size to become a middle-aged woman with smouldering eyes, clad in a Phrygian cap and Arabian clothes.

"You called?" the strange woman asked, Alice gasping again as she gazed at the nebulous form that flickered before her very eyes.

"Who are you?" Alice asked in curiosity and fear, wondering if the woman was a ghost.

"I am Raashida - the genie of the lamp - derived from white, smokeless fire," the woman said in a voice as clear as a bell.

"So you actually exist?" Alice breathlessly asked, "I thought you were only a myth."

"I am many things to many people," Raashida replied, "I don't always appear; I come to whom I choose; and please - do me a favour and pick that up from the floor," she added in a schoolmarmish tone, pointing to the overturned lamp at Alice's feet.

"I've searched for you for years in the hope that we'd meet - and it's only now that you've appeared," Alice said, retrieving the lamp which she instantly placed in her lap.

Raashida's face broke into a smile, but her black, glassy eyes looked concerned.

"My dear - I've only come to you now because I've sensed that it is at this current time that you need my assistance the most," she remarked, dusting down her kaftan as she spoke.

"Oh, I really *do* need your help!" Alice said, fighting back her tears. I struggle with my speech; I struggle with my movements and legs. Cerebral palsy is ruining my life, and I want you to take it away so that I'm able to live a full life like everyone else," she went on, wiping a tear from her cheek that had managed to escape.

Raashida threw Alice a glance to suggest she had not understood why the young woman wanted this change.

"Can you not grant me this wish?" Alice anxiously asked, seeing the dubious look in Raashida's Eastern eyes.

The genie studied the girl's troubled face, Alice finding the silence difficult to bear as she sat, hunched, in her seat losing hope that Raashida would help.

"My dear, I trust that you've now come of age - but you're still very young," Raashia remarked. "These genies in fairytale books one reads as a child are far too ideal.

In reality, just because a genie grants you a wish, doesn't mean to say you'll receive exactly what you want - or that what you desire actually ends up being what you've wished for at first," she added in a cautionary tone, wearing a look to suggest that she bore no ill will.

"I had a huge row with my family just now," Alice said, still reeling from the exchange of acrimonious words between her parents and herself earlier that day. "Because of my cerebral palsy, I'm hardly allowed to go out and to live the life that I want. Sometimes I feel I'm being buried alive - and I want things to change."

Raashida sighed, lowering her incandescent eyes, Alice finding it hard to understand why her wish seemed so awkward to grant.

"OK," the genie finally replied, "I shall grant you your wish - but there's one condition attached," she hesitantly added, realising Alice would not be happy with what she was going to suggest.

"What condition is that?" Alice curiously asked.

"The condition that I take your cerebral palsy away for only a limited time, after which you'll go back to being as you currently are," Raashida replied, Alice failing to grasp what the genie had meant.

"My dear - you're looking confused!" Raashida exclaimed, seeing the puzzled expression on Alice's face.

Alice tightened her grip on the lamp in her lap; her taut, twisted legs beginning to ache as the genie made herself clear.

"You do realise that if I granted your wish and took your cerebral palsy away, you'd become someone else, don't you, my dear?" Raashida went on in a cautionary tone, as Alice clumsily straightened herself up in the chair as best as she could. "The colour of your hair and eyes, and your surname will have changed - and you'll live somewhere else. Your parents will be at their wits end, not knowing where you are, as you'll be classed as a 'person gone missing' - a family member who just disappeared from the scene. It would be cruel to put them through all this anguish for too long; that just wouldn't be fair; so two years from now - on the night of midsummer's eve when the moon appears full - your wish will expire. Any unintentional consequences of this wish will rest entirely on yourself: are you still happy for me to go ahead with the spell?"

Alice peered at Raashida and sighed without giving her warning much thought: all she wanted to do was to live a full life like everyone else, whatever the cost.

"Yes," the young woman firmly replied, reflecting on the limited life she had led for too long.

Raashida shifted her eyes to the silvery lamp before shutting them tight.

"Then, my dear, your wish is my command; and over the next two years, the friends, freedom of lifestyle and job you've always craved shall be yours," she announced, waving her arms in the air, as Alice looked on.

A split second later, the cave began to vibrate, knocking the lamp from Alice's lap to the ground. Then, all of a sudden, the lamp began to light up, as Raashida disappeared in a puff of white smoke, leaving Alice alone once again in the cave.

Alice looked for the lamp which she longed to retrieve, but it was nowhere in sight, having vanished into thin air like Raashida had done. Giving up on her search, she looked down at her legs to find their ungainly stance and pigeon-toed feet proportionately straight; the lingering pain within them through tackling the steps more than an hour ago now a bane of the past.

For the very first time, Alice effortlessly rose from the chair when seeing a set of gold keys attached to a key-ring containing a lamp-shaped logo tagged 'HOME swiftly drop at her feet.' Instinctively knowing they fitted the door of the flat linked to her wish, she picked them up without thought; and placing them in the pocket of her jeans, used her new, able-bodied legs to exit the cave before rapidly descending the steps which once filled her with dread.

Feeling refreshingly free, she passed through the beach towards her new flat, which, she realised, was only a stone's throw away. Minutes later, she reached its front door; and removing the keys from her pocket, unopened the lock, stepping through the threshold and into the hall, where a mirror hung on the wall next to the phone. Alice sidled up to the glass, eyeing her new face and body in pleasure and shock.

"Could this *really* be me?" she incredulously gasped, as a different person stared back, copying each movement and facial expression she made.

She studied her new self again. Gone was the brown, matted hair she could never keep in place; the uncontrollable spasms distorting her body and face had also disappeared. What Alice now saw was a beautiful girl her own age, with long, glossy, blonde hair and speckled, green eyes that sparkled like gems, and whose shoulders were straight and no longer misshapen and hunched.

"No one would recognise me now," she thought with a smile as she walked into the lounge, observing its plush, modern décor and generous size. She had always wanted a flat of her own, and now, her dream had come true.

Alice spent the entire afternoon exploring the rest of her home, the glass-topped cooker and bed with drawers underneath particularly capturing her eyes and filling her with pride.

After having eaten supper she prepared with ingredients found in her larder and fridge, she found it began to grow dark; and at once re-entered the lounge, drawing the curtains across the bay window that captured the view of the sea.

Fetching the remote control from the couch, she switched the television on, to see that the evening news had begun to be aired. She gasped in alarm as she saw her old self appear on the screen - how she had been only hours ago when she entered the cave: the 'cerebral palsy' Alice with stiff, twisted limbs, uncontrollable spasms and eyes that stared into space; whose drab, wispy hair was brown, and whose talking was slurred.

Moments later her parents appeared, sitting, distraught, in the lounge of the house in which Alice had lived; trembling with worry and shock at the loss of their daughter who suddenly vanished and was nowhere to be found. They were huddled together, clinging onto each other for dear life, lest one or the other would suddenly disappear too.

"We're at our wits end," Alice heard her mother sob, staring into the journalist's camera with terrified eyes. "Alice is especially at risk; suffering from cerebral palsy makes her more vulnerable than most. She needs regular medication to ease her condition - drugs she can't do without; how on earth is she going to cope out there all on her own?"

"Because of Alice's condition, 'The Missing Person's Bureau' has already been informed. Alice was able to walk - but not very well. This morning she left the house to calm down after a row with us both - and hasn't come back. An hour since she went missing, we knew that something was wrong - so we called the police. We can only hope and pray she'll be found alive and unharmed," said her father before breaking down; cupping his face in his hands and beginning to cry.

Alice switched the television off; seeing how disturbed and upset her parents had seemed because of her unexplained absence was too much to bear. Before making her wish to be turned into somebody else, she had failed to realise how robbed and distressed her parents would feel if they lost the familiar daughter they both knew and loved: would they be able to shoulder that worry and stress for two further years?

Alice lingered on the couch, spending the next few minutes fighting the guilt which she managed to curb when hearing the telephone ring. Abandoning her seat, she picked up the handset and answered the call. It was her place of work, asking her to be at her desk on Monday morning two hours before she would normally be due to arrive, if nothing had changed. This was because an urgent case had come up: hours ago, a young woman called Alice Sandringham, with cerebral palsy, had strangely disappeared - and had to be found.

🕐 🕐 🕐 🕐 🕐

Alice knew the route to the office where she worked; a four-storey building, with a car park, metres from her flat. It was ironic that the dream of being a social worker for the Missing Person's Bureau had been part of her wish, and that she was now involved in a high risk, missing person's case concerning the absence of herself.

She continued to walk, haunted by posters displaying her old, twisted face - with the word 'MISSING' printed in huge, vibrant letters above - shooting out at her everywhere she looked as she hurried past the police station next to the old people's home.

Reaching the building, she stepped through its doors and entered reception in haste, passing more posters displaying the Alice that others once knew. She averted her eyes, hurrying through the call centre room that led to the Welfare Department where she was to work from now on.

53

"Alice, come in!" Mrs Allen, her supervisor, called, as Alice entered her room; Mrs Allen closing the door before they sat down.

"Alice - I expect you realise why I've called you into work as soon as I could," the supervisor said. "It's concerning Alice Sandringham – the girl with cerebral palsy who suddenly went missing last week. It is now over seventy-two hours since she disappeared, and the police have just called; a search for her will now be carried out. I've chosen you for the case - not because you and Alice share the same name - but because I felt you were the right person for the task. Alice's case is high risk; she is physically disabled, and needs drugs, which - if she's still alive - she's going without. It's a vicious world out there; she could die in a horrible way - and her parents are distraught. They've asked for someone from our unit to visit their house - someone who'd care; and I feel that this person should be *you*."

Alice lowered her eyes; she knew that she had to comply, and this was a job for which she was very well-paid. She now had to face visiting the house from where she stormed out to console the parents that she, herself, had upset. She would have to quiz them on matters regarding herself - and on why they thought she disappeared - questions that she would be able to answer better than anyone else. She would have to pretend to be clueless whilst watching them cry: how could she be so cruelly unkind and two-faced?

"Are you sure I'm the person for this?" she heard herself ask in a feeble attempt to avoid performing the task.

Mrs Allen's wide smile turned into a disapproving frown.

"Alice, this is an order - not a request," the supervisor urged, eyeing the look of reluctance on Alice's face. "You've handled cases like this many times before - so I *know* you'd be able to cope. Now I'll give you the route to the Sandringhams' address so you'll know where it is - and you must go at once," Mrs Allen went on, determined that Alice should deal with the matter in hand.

The supervisor rose from her chair with a firm, tacit nod, Alice following suit - knowing to exit the office and visit her parents in haste. The house was seconds away, and she reached it at once; her stomach churning with dread as she pressed on the bell. Moments later she heard the pounding of footsteps echo from the hall, drawing to a halt as her father opened the door.

"Are you the social worker from 'Missing Person's?'" he asked, staring at Alice through wet, crimson eyes; his broken expression pumping Alice with a feeling of guilt that was difficult to bear.

"Yes," Alice replied, revealing her badge, which her father took from her hand, perusing the details clearly displayed on its front.

"I see that you and my daughter share the same name," he remarked, returning the badge. "No disrespect to yourself, but as soon as I heard someone at the front door, I'd hoped it would be her," he went on, two involuntary tears oozing from his grief-stricken eyes. "Anyway, before we speak in more detail, you'd better come in," he advised, beckoning Alice into the hall where she heard a succession of sobs project from the lounge.

"That's Mary - my wife," he confirmed as the sobbing went on. "She's distraught; has hardly eaten a thing since our daughter went missing last week. I hope you'll be able to help calm her down," he went on as he led Alice into the lounge, where her poor mother sat on the edge of the couch, cupping her head in both hands and continuing to cry.

"Mary," Alice's father gently said, "Alice, the social worker from 'Missing Person's,' is here."

Seeing how broken her mother appeared made Alice feel bad, knowing that the fulfilment of her wish had been the cause; the fear that the ongoing stress may affect the state of both parents' health invading her mind.

"Mary?" her father said again, placing a hand on his wife's trembling arm before helping her rise from the couch to sit by the fire.

"Would you mind sitting here?" he asked, prompting Alice to sit down on the couch as he took a seat in the chair facing his wife's.

"Are you ready to talk?" Alice asked, as she watched Mrs Sandringham wipe her face dry and sit back in her chair.

"Yes," croaked her mother, staring at Alice through tear-ridden eyes.

"My name's Alice - your social worker from the 'Missing Persons' Bureau.' You asked for someone to come round. If your daughter is found, you'll see me again, as *I'd* be the person to ask her a few questions on how she felt when you both saw her last, and on why she may have run away."

"How she *felt*?" her mother exclaimed. "Me and my husband knew only too well how she felt; just like a prisoner - that's how she felt," she went on, her red, swollen eyes riddled with fear. "Because of her condition, all we wanted to do was to keep her from harm; but she accused us of restricting her by keeping her indoors, saying she felt trapped."

"Well, she *did*," agreed Alice, remembering the row between her parents and herself before she stormed out, whilst forgetting that she had transformed.

Both parents' eyebrows shot up as they eyed her in shock.

"How do you know? Did you speak to Alice before

she disappeared?" Mr Sandringham asked, finding Alice's reaction to what his wife said rather strange.

"Oh, no," Alice hastily replied, "I've never met her; never knew her at all - and I'm sure you must have taken her outdoors so as not to leave her feeling hemmed in. But I suppose there were times when she'd longed to be her own person and go out on her own."

"Oh, we *did* take her out - quite often, in fact - and she'd love to visit 'Dryad's Cave,'" Mrs Sandringham defensively said. "But sometimes, a group of young men - who weren't very nice, and looked as if they could be trouble - hung out on the beach. Whenever we'd let Alice out on her own - even sometimes when me or her father went with her - these men would shout across the beach; mock her and taunt her; call her all sorts if names like 'spastic' and 'freak' - and they'd ask her what sin she'd committed in her previous life to be as she was. We'd worry that one day these men would do her some kind of harm if they saw her out on her own. But no matter how many times we'd try to explain this to her, she'd get cross, and argue that her sister used to always be allowed the freedom that she never had - and that she'd feel trapped. Even now, the thought of those men makes our skins crawl - and we wonder if they're the reason why Alice isn't here now."

Alice made no remark on her parents' error of surmise, frustrated at not being able to reassure them that their daughter was alive and unharmed. She understood why they had suspected those rowdy, young men; they were biased, disruptive and loud, and their threats and mocking remarks whenever they saw her would leave her feeling harassed. But now they were probably being questioned on her disappearance by the police - a matter which they knew nothing about and in which they had not been involved.

The interview continued for another ten minutes, until Alice could bear it no more, ending it gently under the excuse that 'time had run out' before exiting the house. At once, she rushed to the beach and headed for the cave, hoping to find the lamp and Raashida again. On her way, she caught sight of the gang of young men that her parents had feared, menacingly waiting on the shore for those to harass. They looked round as they saw her appear; the leader who stirred up their taunts advancing towards the girl whom he used to torment.

"Hi there; I'd like a word," he said as he boldly approached, peering at Alice through curious eyes. "I haven't seen you around here before; are you new to this town?"

Several seconds went by before Alice replied; never before had this young man appeared so polite; but she stayed on her guard.

"Yes," she tersely replied, hoping to end the encounter as soon as she could.

"What's your name?" the gang leader asked, beholding her sleek, golden hair with lascivious eyes.

"Alice," she replied, trying to appear as calm as she could.

"It would be nice to see you again; how about a date?" the gang leader asked, continuing to stare while his followers stood on the shore.

Although Alice should have felt flattered that a member of the opposite gender had found her attractive at last, she felt utterly appalled at how partial this youth had turned out to be. This was not the young man the old Alice had known - but she was the one who had undergone change: how could the same individual be so courteous to one and so vile to somebody else?

"No thanks," she dryly replied, too incensed by the hooligan's bias to consider how rough he could turn if provoked. "But don't worry; I expect there are plenty of other able-bodied fish in the sea!" she added, flouncing away, leaving the young man standing alone to stare at her agape as she resumed her route across the beach.

Seconds later, she entered the cave, making her way to the section of chairs where the old Alice used to spend time. Crouching down on all fours, she scoured the floor of the cave in search of the lamp the old Alice had found. But it was no use; the silvery object was nowhere in sight, and Alice gave up on her search, and rose to her feet.

"Raashida! Where are you?" she desperately called; her voice resounding down the cave. "Raashida, it's Alice! I need to see you again! Raashida, I beg you, please come!"

Half an hour went by during which Alice sat, slumped on the floor of the cave with her head in her hand. Having given up hope that Raashida would come to her aid, she got out her phone, dialling the number of Mrs Allen's office to recount the interview with her parents earlier that day.

"Hello," she heard her supervisor hoot through the phone.

But before Alice spoke, a sudden, powerful force that rocked the whole cave sucked the phone from her hand, sending it flying in a whirlwind of air before landing at her feet. Alice thought that an earthquake was starting to strike, fearing being buried by rocks if the cave were to collapse, or drowned by a huge tsunami rising from the sea, as the cave continued to vibrate, knocking her out of the chair and on to the floor.

The tremor suddenly stopped. Alice rose to her feet, wondering if another would occur as she scanned the floor of the cave in search of her phone. Then all of a sudden, a flash of harsh light assaulted her eyes to make way for a huge cloud of smoke that smothered the core of the cave before shrinking in size. She watched with wide eyes as the cloud changed in shape, transfiguring into a woman who Alice had seen once before.

"Raashida! Is it really you?" the young woman cried, shocked yet relieved that the genie had come back at last.

"Indeed, it is I," Raashida replied, the fumes from the vanishing smoke causing Alice to cough as the genie enlarged.

Alice stared into Raashida's eyes, which wore a look to suggest that she was cross; nevertheless, Raashida had come to her as called, and Alice was grateful for that.

"Oh, Raashida - please help!" Alice desperately said. "I need my wish to be reversed!"

Raashida's eyes looked like fire - turbulent and fierce.

"Did I not warn you of the hidden dangers included in your wish before I went ahead with the spell?" the genie replied; sparks of fiery anger flying out from her eyes. "Did you not heed me when I told you that if I rid you of your cerebral palsy, you'd be classed as a missing person through becoming someone else, and that your parents would be sick with worry that the Alice they knew had disappeared?"

Riddled with guilt, Alice emitted a sigh.

"I heard your warning," she tearfully replied. "But something inside me had hoped the conditions attached to my wish would not be as hard to endure as they turned out to be. Having lived with cerebral palsy has been like a curse, and all I wanted you to do was to take it away," Alice earnestly added, screwing up her eyes. "But now all this doesn't seem right. I can't go on living a lie - with my parents having to be constantly in touch with the Missing Person's Unit and the police. I saw the state they were in earlier today - sick with worry that I could be abducted or dead, and that they may never see me again. When I saw them this morning, I longed to tell them I was safe - that they were looking at *me* and no one else. But they'd never have believed me, because the old Alice they knew and loved had been totally transformed."

"It's a pity you didn't ask me to alter your *parents*, as well; but they probably wouldn't have wished to be transformed," Raashida remarked, still looking displeased.

"And there was one more snag that went with the wish - something you never mentioned in your warning at all," Alice said, feeling resentful and cross. "There's a gang of boys who hang out on the beach who used to harass and taunt me for being like I was. Today the gang leader didn't know who I was - and asked me for a date; but I couldn't forget all the names he'd call me before, like 'spastic,' and 'retard,' and 'boys' nightmare date' - and I know that if he saw the old Alice again, he'd ill-treat and reject me as before. A girl normal from birth would never realise how partial a young man can be depending on the female he sees; but *I* know this only too well - and it really hurts," she went on, feeling sick.

"And yet more conditions will make themselves known before your wish will expire," Raashida remarked, filling Alice with unease.

"I would never have troubled you again had I been able to bear the unforeseen consequences of my wish," Alice earnestly said, as she stood by the wall of the cave feeling foolish and rash.

"Which is why I've visited you again," the genie replied. "Did you think I'd not known what had been going on since I granted your wish? Did you think I hadn't realised how much you'd regretted having changed?"

"Oh, Raashida! I can't express how grateful I am that you've come back to help!" Alice said with a smile.

But Raasida did not smile back, and Alice could see that the look in her eyes was still cold.

"Spare me the sweet, grateful words; they're nothing that I'd understand," said the genie, dismissively waving her hand. "The deeds of a genie are not always good, as you've learned - and after this meeting you'll never see me again. But before I depart, I will reverse your wish and cast another spell."

Alice sighed with relief, but knew not to thank Raashida again, as a sudden strong breeze blew through the cave which lit up and began to vibrate, sucking into its core a tabloid that wrapped around her feet. The breeze fiercely howled as Raashida's dark eyes transformed into lights; her Arabian figure beginning to grow indistinct.

"The crescent moon is still in its cycle," the genie went on as her form continued to fade. "It will be another thirty-six hours before the full moon appears - and it is then that your wish will reverse, and you will transform back into the person you were, and as you were born."

The breeze grew increasingly fierce, sending a chill down Alice's spine as the light that flooded the cave became a deep red.

"And now, I must depart," said Raashida, raising her arms. "I bid you farewell - and if ever you encounter a genie again, I urge you to think before making a wish."

"Goodbye, Raashida," Alice called out, as the genie diminished in size; Alice's words of farewell echoing through the cave as Raashida vanished into mist, leaving the young girl alone to count the last hours during which her new self would exist.

Alice got down on all fours, scouring the floor of the cave in search of her phone, which she found lying at the foot of the chair, hidden beneath a tabloid blown in by the breeze. Picking both items up before rising to her feet, she unfolded the tabloid to see her old self on its front - a snapshot taken by her father before she disappeared.

Letting the newspaper drop, she abandoned the cave, descending the steep, narrow steps that led out to the beach with ease for the very last time.

Deciding to spend her last hours in the comfort of her

flat, Alice passed through the beach, wondering where her old self would be found once the full moon appeared; and as she reached the front door of the home she had craved but knew she would lose, Raashida's warning of the snags attached to a wish coming true re-entered her mind.

She turned the key in the lock and entered the hall, ignoring the supervisor's calls blaring forth from her phone, urging her employee to recount the visit to her parents earlier that day. She spent the afternoon preparing and savouring an overdue lunch, after which she watched programs on her television set in the lounge for the following two hours.

Then, twilight came on, coinciding with the news; her parents' terrified eyes gazing through the screen, pleading with her to come home.

"Don't worry, Mum and Dad - I'll be back very soon!" Alice called out, as if they were able to hear.

Then it grew dark; the new Alice rose from the couch and turned on the light, going over to the window to draw the curtains on her way. Before pulling the chord, she looked out at the landscape beyond; the crescent moon about to change shape, bidding her goodbye.

THE HOUSE WHERE
NOBODY LIVED

Shannon crossed the main road, making her way down the side street that lead to her home. She was new to this part of the land - having moved, three months ago, out of the house in East London that she and her mother had shared for thirty-five years. Quite a few old people's homes and retirement flats could be found in this street - but Shannon's retirement flat was further from the shops - a few streets away.

Turning the corner, she reached the wrong road; this was not the usual route to her home. Her mind had gone totally blank, and having forgotten the exact location of her flat, she had no other choice but to ask someone the way.

"Excuse me!" she called to a woman passer-by.

The woman stopped and looked round, peering at her in silence before drawing near.

"Hello," the woman said as she approached, staring at Shannon through curious eyes.

"Do you know how to get to 'Cornelia Street?' I *thought* I knew the way, but have got a bit lost," Shannon asked in an apologetic tone, cursing herself for forgetting her A-Z when leaving the flat.

"Oh - 'Cornelia Street,'" said the woman with a faint smile. "It's only a stone's throw from here - but you're heading the long way around. "I'm going that way, myself; I'll walk you there, if you like," she went on, as she stared at the bag of provisions that weighed Shannon down, wondering why she was carrying a boatload of items about in an area she did not know well.

"Yes - that would be great," Shannon gratefully said, as the two women started to walk.

"We'll take the short cut," said the woman, leading her down an alley dividing a care home and cottage that stood at the end of the road.

"Are you visiting someone here?" the woman asked. "I haven't seen you in the area before."

"Well actually, I moved here three months ago - but still sometimes get a bit lost whenever I go out," Shannon replied, as they reached the other end of the alley that led to a wood.

"'Cornelia Street' is much quicker to reach if you cut through these woods," the woman advised, as they crossed the road and entered the area of trees.

As they walked deeper into the woods, a small, grassy mound came into view, on which stood an odd-looking house with windows like eyes and a half-moon shaped door that resembled a wide, human mouth.

"That house over there; isn't it strange? I wonder whose it is," Shannon said as they walked past the hill.

"Oh, no one's; it's empty," the woman replied "The council have plans to pull it down. Looks ghostly, doesn't it? - especially at night when it's dark and the street lamps are on."

"It certainly does," Shannon agreed, as the women continued to walk. "Do you know who inhabited it before?"

"It's been vacant for years - even before I moved here," the woman replied as they reached the end of the woods.

"And here is 'Cornelia Street' - closer than you thought," the woman announced, Shannon relieved to find herself back in the street where she lived. "I live in 'Crescent Mews' - two streets away," the woman went on, as the two women came to a corner and drew to a halt.

"Thanks," Shannon said to the woman, getting out her keys. "Sorry to have been so dense; I should know my way around here by now."

"Don't worry," the woman replied. "You'll soon get to know this place like the back of your hand. I'm Emily, by the way - number fifteen - if you fancy dropping by for a chat."

"I'm Shannon," said the other, still feeling abashed about losing her way.

"Have a nice afternoon," Emily said, before turning away to submerge down the neighbouring street which led to her home.

Shannon put down her bag, resting her shoulder and hands before heading home. Once reaching her flat and letting herself in, she unloaded her shopping and stored it promptly away, before spending the rest of the afternoon in the lounge, catching up on her post. Apart from junk mail and three costly bills, a letter from her sister had arrived, mentioning their mother's demise nearly two years ago - before her will had come through - and asking if Shannon would like to keep all the jewellery her mother had owned. Leaving the letter aside, Shannon decided to settle her wretched bills first, writing out checks - as her generation did - to avoid freezing to death, and eating food cold from tin cans through not using the stove.

Sealing the flaps of the envelopes down, she gathered them up, abandoning the lounge for her tiny bedroom at the end of the hall to take out the beige, hooded coat she had bought before selling the house that she and her mother had shared. Donning the coat, she stood by the bed, the window above it providing a view of the woodland she and Emily passed through earlier that day; and on the far right, all on its own, was the ghostly, odd-looking house; its unearthly face drenched in a twilight about to turn black.

"I must send off those cheques straight away," Shannon thought, as she buttoned her coat and placed the bills in her bag; and fetching her keys from the hall, she abandoned the flat, stepping out on the street - now under a black, inky sky dotted with stars.

Recalling her encounter with Emily earlier that day, she remembered having passed a post box on the edge of the woods - near the road where she found herself lost. The one she had used since having moved home was further away; and it was dark, and late, and she had no desire to linger out in the harsh, bitter chill of the night. It would take only minutes to reach the post box if she cut across the woods; the deadline for the payment of her bills was already overdue, and she could not afford to wait another day to send off the cheques.

Pulling on her gloves, she crossed the road to reach the opening of the woods, treading its long, narrow path which led to a thicket of trees. As she reached the dense, shady core, the aura grew bleakly unsafe as the landscape turned black. But a few paces on, she noticed a glazed, milky light exude through the trees, growing increasingly bright as she reached the core's end; and there on the mound, several paces away, stood the weird-looking house she had passed earlier that day; that strange, derelict abode resembling a face.

"But I thought that house was empty, and was going to be pulled down!" Shannon heard herself breathe, bewildered to see that its windows were flooded with light. Drawing nearer to the house to take a closer look, she saw that its dome-shaped, front door was slightly ajar; her ears being met by the mumble of voices inside. Before her a serpentine path wound up the hill, stopping before the front door that was partially shut.

Assuming the house was indwelled by squatters exploiting the council's slowness to act, her curiosity waned; and advancing no further, she turned away from the house, resuming her journey towards the post box now metres away. She continued to walk, grateful for somewhere to live, unlike the squatters who occupied the house through having no home.

Two minutes later, she reached the end of the woods; and fishing the envelopes out of her bag, made her way to the little, red post box that stood by the path. As she posted the cheques, a rustling sound met her ears, causing her to start and abruptly look round.

"What are you doing out here in the dark - all on your own?" Emily exclaimed, drenching Shannon with light from the beam of her torch.

"I could have asked *you* the same thing," Shannon said, eyeing the torch.

"I've taken the car," Emily said, pointing to the little, green vehicle parked across the road. "Don't make your way back to your flat all on your own; I'll drive you back; better still - why don't I drop you back to my house for a chat?"

Shannon secured the woollen scarf around her neck as the frost bit her bones; the inside of Emily's car looking cosy and warm.

"It's freezing out here, so I wouldn't say no," Shannon said, massaging the stiff, frozen fingers under her gloves.

"Then come to the car and jump in; I've got some milk now for a nice cup of tea - and can offer you biscuits, as well," said the other, beckoning her forth; and within seconds, Shannon's fingers warmed up as she sat, ensconced in the passenger's seat, watching the woodland whiz past as Emily talked.

As they drove past the strange, ghostly house, Shannon

saw that its windows no longer shed light; surely those squatters had not already moved out?

"Right - we're practically there," Emily announced, turning the car round a corner and into her street. "Here we are - 'Crescent Mews," she went on, pulling up in her drive. "And before you ask why it all seems so quiet, it's because I live here alone," she added in haste, as the women abandoned the car and entered her house. "My children grew up and left home, and I lost my husband to cancer twelve years ago."

"I'm sorry to hear that," Shannon said.

"Yes - that was a terrible stage in my life - losing Jim - whom I loved very much," Emily replied, as she led Shannon into the lounge before going into the kitchen to put the kettle on.

A few minutes later, Emily returned with the biscuits and two cups of tea which she placed by the couch.

"So, I take it you live alone, too?" she enquired, taking a seat.

"Yes," Shannon said, sipping her tea. "My retirement flat is only big enough for one. I've been single all of my life, and have lived with my mother up until the time she passed away. After she died, I sold the house and moved here."

"Where was the house?" Was it far from where you live now?" Emily enquired, helping herself to a chocolate biscuit from the plate.

"Yes, it *was* quite a distance from here - Wanstead, East London - near Essex," said Shannon, draining her cup.

"Yes, that *is* rather far," Emily remarked, eyeing Shannon closely as she spoke. "Does anyone you know live around here?"

"No," Shannon said, unsure if she liked being asked. "I came here because when looking for somewhere to live, I liked the look of the flat; it seemed better than any of the other flats that I viewed. I'm not sure about the view from my bedroom window, though; the look of that house on the hill gives me the creeps."

"Oh, I wouldn't let *that* put you off!" Emily said. "That house has been empty for years - and as I've already pointed out, it will soon be demolished - and then it will be gone. Anyway, I think that those woods look quite picturesque. What's the matter?" she quizzically asked, noticing the puzzled expression on her guest's face.

"Are you *sure* no one lives in that house?" Shannon asked, remembering her walk through the woods earlier on.

"One hundred per cent," the other firmly replied. "I've lived in this area for twenty-five years - and know it like the back of my hand. The last people living in that house were a very old couple - and when the wife died, the husband moved into a home; the house has been empty since then."

"That's rather strange," Shannon remarked, "because earlier this evening, as I cut across the woods, its door was ajar, and I saw the lights on in both its windows upstairs. I also thought I heard voices coming from inside. I thought, maybe, squatters had moved in; although squatters use candles - and the light coming from the windows didn't look much like candlelight to *me*; it looked like the light from a bulb."

"Well, *I* didn't see any light coming from the house when we passed it just now; it looked totally unoccupied to *me*," Emily replied, putting down her cup.

Shannon mutely looked down. She had hoped that Emily would agree to go with her to the woods to look at the house - but could tell by her host's reaction that she would not come.

"You must come here again to have lunch - or we could both meet up for a meal at 'Willow Tree Lane;'

it has plenty of places to eat.".," Emily said, throwing Shannon a smile.

"Yes - that would be nice," Shannon blandly replied, finding her host too nosey and forceful by far.

Seconds of silence went by. Shannon focussed her eyes on the tray by the couch, let down that Emily had not revealed more about the history of the strange, ghostly house in which nobody lived.

"You look tired; do you want to go home?" Emily asked, sensing Shannon's unease.

"Yes, I *do* feel quite tired. I didn't sleep well last night; had to settle some outstanding bills. I had better go back to my flat and catch up on my rest," Shannon said, as both women rose from their seats.

Emily offered to drive her guest home - but Shannon declined, making her way back to the flat on her own. She took off her coat before entering the lounge where she sat, gathering her thoughts. The full moon blinked through the curtains she had drawn to block out the night, as she pondered on the settee, regretting her decision to move into the flat without thinking things through. The flat itself was ideal, but the area in which it was placed had an aura she disliked; with its gardens of seasonal flowers adorning abodes that looked neatly middle class, and its array of groomed, tree-lined streets, restaurants and shops; attractive to look at, yet dowdy within - and Emily's dismissive impatience and glib social skills embodied it well.

Switching off the light, Shannon went into the bedroom to retire for the night. Before drawing the curtains, she peered through the window at the strange house on the hill, now completely unlit and with no sign of life. Yet only hours ago as the sky was growing dark, she saw light flooding though its eyes - and whether it had been voices of squatters or residents that she heard streaming from its mouth, it was hard to believe that the house had been derelict for years. Behind her superficial smiles, Emily, for one, had dismissively refused to believe that even squatters could have moved in.

But Shannon was sure that her mind was not playing tricks. She knew there was someone in that house when she had passed it earlier on; and if Emily would not go with her into the woods to see who it was, she would go there alone - and resolve to seek out the truth.

🕐 🕐 🕐 🕐 🕐

Dawn had yet to arrive, and the full moon was out. Shannon switched on her torch as she walked through the trees; their leaves now a reddish gold carpet coating a ground eclipsed by the night. Feeling cold, Shannon paused to wrap the thick, woollen scarf she had kept in her bag round her neck, in the hope that no louts or wild dogs would career her way.

Reaching the end of the wood's murky core, she came within sight of the house, still looking as empty and dead as Emily had believed; no light in its grim, glassy eyes; its arched, mocking mouth firmly shut. Maybe the squatters were sleeping elsewhere for the night; but a curious urge nagged Shannon not to turn back.

Gripping the strap of her bag, Shannon walked on, the house growing large as she neared the damp, grassy mound. Drawing to a halt, she wound the beam of her torch up the serpentine path that stole up to the arch-shaped, front door, perusing its grey coat of paint and rusty, brass lock. She listened for voices inside, but everything was quiet, except for the hoot of an owl from a far-away tree.

All of a sudden she found herself climbing the hill, ascending the narrow, coiled path that led to the door.

In seconds, she came to the top, and peered through a window on the ground floor into one of the rooms. There was furniture inside: a wooden table surrounded by chairs, a sink, a cooker, a clock, and a picture on the wall; whilst the hands of the clock had not stopped and displayed the right time.

She started in shock, dropping her torch as a light from the window above suddenly appeared, followed by a strong gust of wind that forced open the door, letting her inside. The hall was dark and unlit, and she switched on her torch, clicking the door shut behind her as she stepped in.

She stole down the hall, running the beam of the torch up the stairs and over the walls in search of a socket of light. Spotting one on the wall past the stairs a few paces ahead, she pressed down its switch; but no light came on, and she had no choice but to keep on her torch as a guide.

Creeping into the room next to the one with the cooker and sink at the end of the hall, she discovered a couch at its rear, whilst an old fashioned television set perched on a chair was positioned on a rug directly in front. She stared at the contents and frowned, surprised that a derelict house contained items that had not been cleared.

She abandoned the room and returned to the hall, stealing upstairs to explore the rest of the house. Seeing that the light from the room upstairs was still on, she switched off the torch. Then all of a sudden, she heard a child start to cry. The bawling went on, growing increasingly loud as she drew near the room. She slowly edged open the door, which deafeningly creaked as she sidled inside, staring at what she could see through wide, disturbed eyes.

Covering two thirds of the room was a large, double

bed on which a girl approximately nine years of age lay face down, repeatedly screaming out "Stop!" amid frequent sobs. Standing before the young girl was a man of about thirty-five, with a bristly beard, dressed in clothes belonging to men of the past. A stick was clasped in his hand which he angrily raised, before beating the child with such force that she cried out in pain.

"Stop attacking that girl - or I'll call the police!" Shannon instantly cried; her face growing crimson with rage as she reached for the stick. But the man neither heard nor looked up; Shannon's hand merely sliding through his as she tried to step in.

Determinedly cross, she attempted to pull the girl from the bed, only to slip through the frightened child's arm when she stretched out her hand. She gasped in utter dismay as she realised that though she could see the man and the terrorized girl, they could not see *her* - neither being even aware she had entered the room.

There was only one answer to this: the man and the scared, abused child were already dead, probably having lived in the house ages ago - which accounted for the anachronistic aura that they conveyed. Shannon withdrew from the edge of the bed and backed out of the room, as the child continued to wail on receiving another hard strike from the stick in the angry man's grasp. Switching her torch back on, Shannon hurried downstairs, slipping outdoors through the half-moon, front door as fast as she could.

Making her way down the path, she saw that the sky was beginning to turn light, transforming from ebony black to crimson and gold. Retracing her steps through the woods, she returned to her flat; the terrified eyes of the child haunting her mind as she took off her coat and entered the kitchen in shock.

"They're both only ghosts, who must both have died

ages ago and can't do any harm," she pondered out loud, pouring herself a cup of hot, sweetened tea.

She abandoned the kitchen at once and entered the lounge with her cup, to see that outside it was light. She made sure to drink down her tea whilst it was hot, before resting the cup, and drawing open the curtains to let in the sun. She looked up as she saw a woman wave through the pane - a woman retired, and getting on in years, who lived on her own, like herself.

"Shannon! Hello!" called the woman from outside in a voice that could barely be heard. "Have you got a minute? Are you busy right now?"

Shannon felt her mouth drop, as Emily hovered outside; her nose pressed up against the glass as if it were glued.

"Oh no," Shannon muttered in dread, throwing Emily an artificial smile. "She's expecting me to invite her into the flat. Right now she's all smiles - but if I say the wrong thing, how long will it be before I see her other side?"

"Just a minute!" she called, reluctantly going into the hall to open the door.

Emily's face beamed into hers as the door edged steadily back; and a few minutes later, the former was perched on the couch, clasping a mug of hot tea, with Shannon at her side. Shannon was glad she had tidied the flat as she watched her guest's eyes inquisitively circulate the room, looking for something untidy to report to her neighbours as soon as she left.

"Are you settling into the area OK?" Emily asked, searching Shannon's face with prying, penetrative eyes.

"Well, I've only been here a few months - so I suppose I'll get used to it in time," Shannon vaguely replied, feeling more out of place than she dared to let on.

"I find your outlook quite strange," Emily remarked. "You're the very first person I've asked who hasn't taken to this area as soon as they'd moved in. Is there anything about it that you don't particularly like?"

Shannon thought. It was hard to express why she was not keen on the area to which she had moved; it just felt out of place. The only tangible reason to enter her mind was the menacing view of that strange, eerie house from her flat. Remembering how Emily closed up when she mentioned the house the previous night, Shannon took a deep breath before broaching the subject again:

"I had another look at that house," she gingerly began, wondering how Emily would react.

Emily put down her mug.

"Which one?" she enquired, not knowing which house Shannon meant.

"That house on the hill - the one in the woods that you told me the council were planning to pull down," Shannon said, hoping her guest would not alter the subject again.

"When?" Emily asked, seeming suddenly tense.

"I went there this morning - just before dawn," Shannon said, bracing herself for what she was going to recount.

Emily's eyes slid down Shannon's face; their expression indignant and cold.

"Oh, well; perhaps it was better that you went there and saw for yourself you'd been wasting your time - because I bet you found no sign of life," the former remarked in a tone of dissent.

"Actually, I *did*," Shannon firmly replied, determined that she was heard out.

"What do you mean? Emily snapped, Shannon seeing her true colours much sooner than she thought.

"When I got to the house, it was dark. I peered through the window and saw furniture inside," Shannon began, in the hope that her host would take what she told her on board. "Then suddenly, the front door blew open and I entered the hall with my torch. No lights were on, but I saw that the room at the back was furnished, as well. After that, I went up the stairs, and saw a light on in one of the rooms—"

Emily did not interrupt; but the hostile look in her eyes had not gone away, as she sat on the couch, letting Shannon talk on.

"I entered the room, which looked like a bedroom, and saw two people inside - a man and a child. The child was lying face down on the bed, while the man held a stick. He was beating the girl with the stick, and making her cry. I begged him to stop - but he couldn't see or hear me; *neither* of them could; I think they must have been ghosts. They certainly seemed to be something out of the past."

Emily tightened her lips; Shannon feeling unnerved by the hate in her eyes.

"Those who have to dig deep don't always like what they find. I'm amazed that a woman of your age hasn't learnt to mind her own business and leave well alone - long before now!" Emily snapped, as she suddenly got up, marching her way to the door with her hands on her hips."

"I can't understand why you've such a problem with this," Shannon said as she rose from her seat, finding Emily's reaction a little bit odd. "How *can* what I've told you bother you so much, when you firmly believe that the house has been empty for years - and that it still is?"

"Anyone who dares to cross me and push me too far, I cut them out," Emily barked, turning back. "But you always get one who'll come along and shatter the peace. And don't bother coming to the door; I'll see myself out!" she went on, storming out of the lounge to slam the door shut as she exited the house.

Shannon stared through the window agape, watching

her host disappear down the pavement outside. She regretted having mentioned her visit to the house and what she had seen after venturing inside. She wondered, too, why Emily was so reluctant to talk about the house; and indeed, having pressed the subject in Emily's presence had lost her a friend. Finding another acquaintance would prove more easily said than done, especially in an area like this, where the inhabitants were aloof, and there were hardly any clubs for her to join.

Shannon sat back down on the couch; and with her knuckles tucked under her chin, mulled over her new, retired life. She told herself that she had moved only three months ago and that she would grow used to the area in time; but her instincts strongly demurred, warning her that she would never assimilate into a place of this kind, no matter how long she would stay. She remembered having seen an estate agent's firm in "Willow Tree Lane" while out shopping a few weeks ago, and wondered if they would be able to help her move on. But right now, this could wait - at least one more day; for today she would be travelling to London, where she once lived; the town she loved and where she and her sister were born.

She rose from the couch and took out some cash from the drawer which she placed in her purse, and fetching her holdall, she packed a few items, including her toothbrush and socks. Since Emily would not be treating her to lunch, she would now be treating herself. She would dine at a restaurant in "Bloomsbury Square," and stay at a hotel tonight before travelling back.

Pushing her thoughts of Emily aside, she took out her phone; and once ordering a cab, she fetched her coat from the hall.

The next morning, Shannon woke up refreshed, sliding out of a bed that the maid would remake, to step into a bathroom that smelt of fragrant fresh air. After her shower, she switched on the kettle; its whirr failing to numb the buzz of the streets of West London outside. Sipping her Darjeeling tea, she gazed through the window onto the pavements below; scattered with tourists and those on their travels to work, whilst busy, black taxis pulled up on the kerb to pick wealthy customers up.

Planning to go down for breakfast at quarter past nine, she abandoned the window and turned on the television set opposite her bed. On some of the channels, 'Breakfast TV' was still airing the regional news; but BBC2 transmitted a programme about past events in the area where Shannon now lived - Newton St Faith.

Shannon watched the programme agape, as the ghostly house on the hill appeared on the screen; and increasing the volume of the set, listened to what was being said with riveted ears. She could not believe what she heard when the narrator revealed that the house was said to be haunted by ghosts from the past, and that seventy years ago, an uncle murdered his nine-year-old niece in the heart of the bedroom upstairs. Shannon's blood turned to ice as a snapshot of him and the girl appeared on the screen: they were the same man and child she had seen when she entered the house before dawn the previous day.

She saw by the television guide that the documentary was not being aired in Newton St Faith, finding it strange that no one in that area had mentioned the history of the house. She was still bemused by Emily's negative reaction to having been told that a man and a child were seen within its walls, wondering how her acquaintance would respond to the documentary being aired.

The programme ended at nine forty-five - too late for

breakfast downstairs. Shannon switched off the television set and got out her coat. She had planned to spend the day at the British Museum, where perhaps she could eat an early lunch.

Abandoning her room, she made her way down to the lounge; and as she sat by the window, trying to decide where to eat, a woman approached, taking the padded, grey seat next to her own. Shannon abruptly looked up as she noticed how similar to Emily this woman appeared; having the same affectations and probing look in her eyes, which threw Shannon a glance to suggest she was staring too much.

"Forgive me for staring," said Shannon, dropping her eyes. "It's just that you look so much like a person I know, that for a moment I thought you were her."

The woman eyed her again; and for a few seconds, Shannon thought she would rise from her seat and scurry away. The woman's expression, however, grew less severe, and feeling less ill at ease, Shannon threw her a smile.

"Oh, I see," the woman replied; her manner remaining aloof. "You're not the first person to say that to me; that's because I have a twin seconds younger than me."

"Her name's not Emily, by any chance?" Shannon jokingly asked, as she thought of the petulant woman who gave her short shrift.

"Actually, it *is*," the other replied; her eyes growing wide in surprise. "Where does she live?"

"Norfolk - Newton St Faith - where *I* live, as well. She told me she'd lived there for twenty-five years," Shannon said.

"Does she live in 'Crescent Mews - near the woods?" the woman enquired, almost staring Shannon out.

"Yes - actually, she *does* - number fifteen!" Shannon exclaimed.

The woman suddenly went quiet, as if something were wrong.

"How utterly strange," she remarked, after a pause. "That's *definitely* her. What a coincidence - coming across a friend of my twin sister here - in this hotel!"

Shannon lowered her eyes as she thought of how Emily turned cold the previous day.

"Well, to be honest," she began, putting the other woman right, "I've only lived in Newton St Faith for three months - and don't really know your twin sister that well."

"Oh, I see; you're new to Newton St Faith. Oh, well - I suppose you'll probably be friends with Emily in time," the woman replied, unaware that her twin sister had made it clear that she would not see Shannon again.

Shannon did not reply; she threw the woman an uneasy smile, wondering how well the two twin sisters got on. The woman scanned Shannon with her eyes, bemused as to why she went quiet; Shannon feeling the need to shatter the ice.

"My name's Shannon, by the way," she finally announced.

"I'm Sarah," the woman replied, wondering if Shannon would suddenly clam up again.

"I came down too late for breakfast today. I was watching a documentary this morning on BBC2 - up in my room; it was about a house on a hill that's said to be haunted - in Newton St Faith," Shannon said, trying her best to converse.

Sarah's expression immediately changed, and Shannon wondered if she had said anything wrong. Following a silence, Sarah looked down, hiding her obvious disquiet with a self-conscious smile before looking up.

"I know what happened in that house only too well," she eventually said, swallowing hard and wringing her hands before going on. "It was a good job Emily hadn't known the documentary was going to be aired; she would have been terribly upset if she had."

"Well, I know it seemed to upset her whenever I mentioned the house," Shannon said, remembering how hostile towards her Emily had turned.

Sarah let out a sigh; the look in her eyes now one of reflective regret.

"It's nothing she'll ever talk about," she began, sighing again, "The number of times we've tried to get her to open up, but the subject upsets her too much. The family know what happened to her in relation to the house."

"So, she's *been to* the house?" Shannon asked in surprise, realising Emily knew more about the abandoned abode than she cared to admit.

"Emily used to *live* in that house - but she and her family were only there for just over a year," Sarah declared, as Shannon listened with intent.

"When did they move in?" Shannon asked; keen to hear more.

"About thirteen years ago - shortly before her husband passed away," Sarah sadly replied, lowering her eyes once again.

"Her husband died from cancer, didn't he?" Shannon tentatively asked, remembering what Emily had said when she visited her house.

"That's what you may have been told, but it isn't the truth," Sarah said, looking pained. "Her husband, Jim, died from a totally different cause."

"What cause was that?" Shannon asked, wondering why Emily had lied.

Sarah evaded her eye, hesitating before she replied.

"It was all so tragically sad," began Emily's twin, inhaling deeply before going on. "Rumours of that house being haunted were, actually, true. Two ghosts inhabited it while Emily and her family were there - a middle-aged man and a child. I saw them once when I stayed round the house for the night. The girl had long, golden hair

82

and terrified eyes, and the man looked evil to the core; he had a beard and was holding a stick which looked like a cane. I didn't see them when Emily and the family were there, but during the night - when I was alone in the bedroom upstairs. The man looked angry, and called the girl's name - which I think was Molly-Mae - who then appeared by the bed. Molly-Mae started to wail; then they both disappeared. They haunted the family non-stop; never left them in peace."

"And what did that have to do with your brother-in-law's death?" Shannon asked, perceiving Sarah's distress through her dark, probing eyes.

"Quite a lot," Sarah firmly replied. "Jim had a bad heart, and needed a quiet life to survive - which he had before he and the family moved to Newton St Faith."

Sarah paused and looked down, aware that recounting the cause of Jim's death evoked memories of pain.

"When he and my sister moved into the house, they saw the two ghosts - but neither Molly-Mae nor the man appeared to see *them*---."

"The girl in the documentary this morning was called Molly-Mae. Was the man called Joe Black? - because that's what the narrator said he was called," Shannon cut in, remembering not having been seen by the ghosts in the house the previous day, despite having seem them.

"Yes, it was," Sarah said, looking strained. "He was a relation; Molly-Mae's uncle, I think."

"Yes - that's what the narrator had said," Shannon exclaimed.

"Anyhow," Sarah resumed, feeling mere names were not linked to what had occurred. "As time went on, Emily's family became visible to Joe and Molly-Mae - and as soon as they were, the ghosts wouldn't leave them alone. They would pester them night and day - but mainly at night---"

"Go on," Shannon urged, still curious to know how Emily's husband had died.

Sarah sighed, and then paused, finding the tale of Jim's death hard to recount.

"It was on New Year's Eve night - six months after Emily and the family moved into the house," Sarah began, swallowing hard. "Victoria - Emily's daughter - had celebrated her birthday the previous day; I think she'd turned eight - and Jim had just tucked her in bed before bidding her goodnight. As Jim left her room to go back downstairs, he heard someone cry, and saw Molly-Mae in tears at the foot of the stairs. He rushed down to the hall where she stood to ask what was wrong - but her ghost disappeared."

"What happened next?" Shannon asked, sensing Sarah's unease.

"Jim hurried into the lounge where Emily sat, watching TV. '"Emily!"' he called, "The child has reappeared; I saw her at the foot of the stairs a moment ago!' Emily got up from the couch, and they both ran into the hall to see Joe at the top of the stairs, holding a knife. '"Molly-Mae!"' he furiously called, glaring down at the steps— and it was then that he saw Emily and Jim in the hall, and turned his anger on *them*. '"What have you done with my niece?"' he screamed out. '"What has she said to you both about me? I know you've hidden her away - and I want to know where!"' he shouted again, waving his fist. '"I know your daughter is sleeping upstairs; is Molly-Mae in her room?"' Emily and Jim told Joe to get lost - but that made the situation worse. '"Well, if neither of you will tell me where Molly-Mae is, I'll find out for myself,"' Joe Black said; and as soon as Emily and Jim saw him head for Victoria's room, they rushed up the stairs - scared that his presence would leave Victoria disturbed if she saw him burst in. But by the time they'd both entered her room, they found him already inside - standing over her bed with the knife as she cried out in fear. Emily tried to reassure Jim that Joe was only a ghost, and that using the knife on Victoria would have no effect; but seeing his daughter so scared and distraught upset him so much, that his heart suddenly gave way - and that's how he died."

"And that's when Emily and the children decided to move out?" Shannon cut in.

"Yes," Sarah confirmed, "but it took a quite while for the house to be sold. An old couple bought it in the end - and that's when Emily and the family moved to 'Crescent Mews.'"

Shannon imagined how scared Victoria must have felt when she saw Joe Black's ghost leaning over her bed with a knife.

"And how is Victoria now; is she OK?" she gingerly asked, hoping her question would not be considered too personal to pose.

"Well, she *seems* OK now - but seeing Joe's ghost burst into her room with the knife has left her feeling threatened by the world - even today - and she's needed regular, intensive counselling for years," Sarah sadly replied, lowering her eyes.

"What a malevolent ghost; look at the damage he's caused," Shannon said, angry at what she had heard.

Sarah abruptly looked up, with eyes full of rage.

"*Of course* Joe Black's ghost was malevolent!" she bitterly cried. "If he could ill-treat his own niece the way he did every second of the day, he's *bound* to mean people harm!"

Shannon forced a faint smile, feeling uneasy at Sarah's eruptive response.

"I must go; there's an exhibition at the British Museum that I came here to see," she hastily announced, sensing she had pushed her questions on Jim's demise a little too far. Sarah looked on in sedentary silence, as Shannon got up from her seat, eyeing Emily's twin with a cautious unease.

"Nice meeting you, Sarah," said Shannon, seizing her bag.

"OK then, Shannon; have a nice day - and when you see Emily again, give her my love," Sarah tersely replied; her manner making it clear she had no more to say.

Feeling a little shamefaced, Shannon turned away, hurriedly heading for the desk to hand in her key.

🕐 🕐 🕐 🕐 🕐

Shannon trudged up the serpentine path and entered the house. The light from its window upstairs had been on since the previous day - twenty-four hours since she had returned from her trip.

With the aid of her torch, she searched the rooms and the lobby downstairs, and discovering no sign of life, focussed her mind on the ramshackle storey above. Reaching the top of the stairs, she switched off her torch, eyeing the shower of light streaming forth from the bedroom in which she had seen the two ghosts when venturing into the house two mornings ago.

As hostile as Emily and Sarah had been, she felt Joe Black's ghost had mercilessly blighted their lives; driving Emily's daughter to mental ill heath, and her husband into a bleak, premature grave. Even Sarah - as merely the sister and aunt - appeared scathed by the irreparable damage that Joe Black had caused; and had the elderly wife who moved into the house after Emily moved out simply died of old age?

But Shannon surmised that Joe's ghost had killed this wife too, and felt that the ongoing pain he was causing to others had gone on too long. She hoped he would notice her presence this time, as she pulled out a can of aerosol spray from her bag, ready to enter the room where she saw him before; she was going to tackle this ghost and put him through hell.

As her hand met the doorknob, she heard Molly-Mae start to cry, and removing the cap from the can, bustled into the room, ready to pounce. Joe Black's ghost sat in the corner, on the dressing table stool, with the stick in his grasp; his eyes transfixed on his niece who lay cowering on the floor, centimetres away.

"Please, Uncle Joe, don't beat me again! I promise I'll do as you say!" begged Molly-Mae, amidst intermittent sobs of terror and pain.

Joe widened his eyes in a rage, while raising the stick.

"Speak when you're spoken to, girl!" he furiously yelled, ready to strike Molly-Mae with the stick once again. "I'll stop beating you when I see fit - now do as I say, and lie flat!"

"Drop that stick *now*! Drop it, or I'll use this can of spray!" Shannon cried, brandishing the can.

But the ghosts were still unaware of her presence in the room, Joe's ghost oblivious to the attack she was going to carry out. As the stick was about to descend on Molly-Mae's legs, Shannon homed in, pressing down hard on the button of the aerosol can. She let out a frustrated sigh as the spray produced no effect, passing through Uncle Joe's face and on to the wall. Desperate to stop Molly-Mae being beaten again, she attempted to drag the child from the floor, but her hands slipped through the girl's arms that she wanted to seize.

The stick landed down hard on Molly-Mae's legs, and the girl started crying again. Cross about failing to stop the assault, Shannon drew nearer to Joe, before trying to strike him hard on the head with the can; but it merely slipped through his form as the stick continued to bruise

Molly-Mae's legs whist she cried out in pain, begging him to stop.

Shannon tried to catch his attention by hurling the can against the wall, and upturning a chair that had stood next to the bed. She began to shout insults at Uncle Joe's ghost, who heedlessly carried on beating his terrified niece. But bearing in mind that the ghosts were aware of Emily's family's presence after a while, she refused to give up, kicking the can around the room as hard as she could.

It was then that Joe's ghost suddenly looked round, dropping the stick in surprise; his eyes darting around the room to meet Shannon's own. Shannon marched up to him with her hands on her hips and grabbed the stick from the floor, snapping it wildly in half with resolute force.

"Oh, silly me; why didn't I think?" she furiously cried. "I should have used this stick to hammer you with instead of snapping it in half.

Uncle Joe got up from the stool; his niece fleeing to the opposite corner of the room.

"Who the hell do you think you are - barging into another person's house? Look what you've done to my stick!" Joe angrily yelled.

"And what about the damage *you've* caused? You've inflicted nothing but misery on others over the years!" Shannon snapped back.

"And what business is all this of *yours*?" Joe furiously asked. "This has nothing to do with you - so stop interfering and shift from this house before I throw you out of here myself!"

Uncle Joe lifted his arm; his hand forming into a fist, as Shannon reached for the can lying by the wall. In seconds the spray was released, only to pass through Joe's face once again, causing Shannon's fear of being attacked to subside.

"You can't hurt me; you're dead! Try and frighten me all you like, but it's not going to work, as I'm not scared of ghosts - so hard luck!" she aggressively yelled.

Joe's fist passed through her jaw as he tried to strike her down.

"You Missed! Hard luck on *that* score, as well!" she derisively cried, laughing with glee.

"Get out of here, you old bitch!" Uncle Joe yelled.

"Make me!" Shannon screamed back, as his niece remained crouched in the corner of the room, too scared to intervene.

"I know about you," Shannon cried, pointing a captious finger at the male ghost. "You abused and murdered your niece decades ago - right here, in this room. It just shows how pathetic you are - targeting a child. Emily and her children had to move out because you wouldn't leave the family alone soon after they moved here. You hounded her husband to death, and traumatised her daughter, Victoria, for life when you entered her room, brandishing a knife on that New Year's Eve night. An elderly couple moved in after Emily moved out, and soon after that, the wife died: did you happen to kill *her* as well? Do you terrorise everyone you see, and drive them away? Is that why the house is unoccupied *now*?" she went on, narrowing her eyes.

"I told you, you meddlesome bitch - this is not your concern!" Uncle Joe snarled, trying to cow Shannon with his size by drawing up close. "Now get out of this house before I make *you* a victim, as well!"

"Do you really rely on these four walls that much?" Shannon enquired with a smirk. "Well, I'm sorry you do - as I've news you'll be interested to hear."

Joe Black's ghost did not reply, but his eyebrows were raised. A few seconds went by before Shannon went on, during which she continued to gloat.

"Your precious house will soon be no more; the council are going to pull it down - which will mean that you'll go down with it - hurray!" she resumed with a snort.

"You're lying!" Joe cried, his threatening expression changing to one of alarm. "You're nothing but a meddlesome, old woman - claiming to be sure of affairs she knows nothing about!"

Shannon opened her bag, taking out the clip of a newspaper article published the previous week.

"And the council and paper reporters are lying, as well, I suppose?" she snapped back, holding up the cutting before Joe's incredulous eyes. "So do Newton St Faith a favour; go back to your grave forever - and disappear *now;* and even if you don't, you soon will when the house is smashed down: has the penny dropped *now*?"

Uncle Joe opened his mouth and let out a roar; not one of wrath, but one of frustration and fear. Shannon watched as his form became still, vanishing into thin air as his niece followed suit. She took one last look at the room, wondering if the ghosts would return to the house before it came down; and placing the can of spray and newspaper clip back in her bag, she stepped through the door, clicking it shut amidst thoughts of what had just passed.

As she walked down the stairs with the aid of her torch, the light in the bedroom went out, and slipping through the front door under a rusty gold sky, she descended the serpentine path, and made her way home.

As she entered the hall, a note from Emily was lying on the mat, expressing how sorry she was for her outburst before Shannon went away, and asking if they could be friends all over again. Maybe they could, but only if Shannon refrained from mentioning the house where Emily once lived - the house where her husband had died twelve years ago. Shannon was glad she had frightened the two ghosts away, but it was too late; the damage to Emily's family had long since been done - and besides, the house would soon be pulled down and no longer exist.

Shannon placed the note to one side, and leaving on her coat, she removed the aerosol can and torch from her bag before putting them away. Once shutting her drawer, she peered through her bedroom window further down the hall, and saw that the house on the hill showed no sign of life; no light streaming forth from its eyes; its mouth fully closed; it was now as Emily had wished it had been - harmless and void.

Shannon felt sorry for Emily now that she knew what had happened to her family and herself. What a vile, evil man Molly-Mae's uncle had been. Then that same, intangible feeling hit her again, reminding her how out of place she still felt in the area to which she had moved.

"No - Emily and I will never be friends," she decidedly thought, exiting her bedroom in haste.

For Shannon had made up her mind; she was going to the estate agent's firm in "Willow Tree Lane" and make plans to move out. She was going back to East London where she would spend the rest of her days; the land of no airs and graces; no unseen ghosts.

THE FRUITS OF LABOUR

Skye headed back home after work, feeling wronged and misunderstood - but most of all drained. She stopped at the church by the bridge on her way, to gather her nerve: how was her mother going to react to her losing her job? It had not been Skye's fault; she had not realised that voicing her fears to her manager and colleague about answering the phones would be wrong. Now she was working her notice; then in a few weeks, she would be out - joining the ranks of the jobless, looking for work.

After checking her iPod for texts, she continued her journey back home; Steven Hayes - her eight-year-old cousin - and his mother would be coming to the house for a Halloween tea.

"Penny for the guy," called a gaunt-looking boy on the verge of his teens, as she came to the bridge; and ignoring the two pound coin that remained in her purse, she grew heedlessly deaf and walked on, reaching the other end of the bridge to enter a side street of stalls selling pumpkins, fake blood and face masks to mark Halloween.

Remembering her mother's request to bring home a cake, she stopped at a stall selling Halloween snacks that included Frankenstein cup cakes and iced eyeball buns.

"Would you like to buy one of these Dracula cakes; they're an absolute snip at three pounds," the stallholder said as he saw her approach.

"Do you have any cakes that cost a pound less?" Skye enquired, remembering that two pounds was all the spare cash she had left.

"Two fifty - and it's yours," the stallholder said, reducing the price.

Skye looked down and sighed, cursing herself for leaving the money to cover the cost of the cake for the supper behind; and having been axed from her job, thought it best not to draw any money out of her bank.

"On second thoughts, I'll give it a miss; I'm trying to slim," she uneasily said, abandoning the stall for the corner shop seconds away.

Entering the store and browsing its shelves in the hope of finding something for fifty pence less, she found the cakes that it sold were more dear than the stall's; but further down the aisle, on the reduced items shelf, stood a sizeable cake in the form of a ghost for only two pounds - which should stay fairly fresh if consumed on the day it was bought. Skye seized the box with both hands after emptying her purse; the two pound coin growing warm in her grasp as she made for the till.

As she neared the front of the shop, two people walked in - the male employer who had told her to leave and the sly female colleague who roused his action by stabbing her, cruelly, in the back. Neither the man nor the woman said hello, despite making it tacitly clear that they saw her retreat; the smirk on the woman's smug face making Skye squirm as her eyes stared into her own. Aware that they would not respond had she greeted them first, Skye averted her eyes, sidling up to the till with unease where she paid for the cake with the coin that she could not replace.

Hurrying out of the shop, she continued her journey back home, removing the price from the box that protected the cake before entering the house.

"Cousin Skye!" Steven called, darting into the hall as he heard her come in. "Me and Mum came here early; is that for our tea?" he avidly asked, pointing to the cut-price cake in the young woman's grasp.

"Yes, it is," Skye replied, hiding her fears with a smile as she put down the box to take off her coat.

"Your mum said we could have our tea in this room," Steven said, once Skye picked up the cake and followed him into the lounge.

Steven dived on to the couch, whilst Skye placed the boxed cake on a table in the corner of the lounge amongst the various Halloween treats that her mother had prepared.

"Will you read me a nursery rhyme?" Steven asked, pointing to the sleek-covered book on the shelf by the hearth.

"Which one would you like me to read?" Skye half-heartedly asked, fetching the book before taking a seat beside Steven on the settee.

"Any will do; *you* can choose," her cousin replied, as he waited for her to begin with wide, eager eyes.

Skye opened the book, turning its pages with traumatised hands; her mind plagued by the dread of informing her mother her job had been axed.

"Have you found one yet?" Steven asked, as she flicked through the book, pained by its sketches of pumpkins, Jack Horner and mice.

Skye paused at the page sprawled with drawings of churches and fruit; the mention of debt seizing her mind as she read the first line - and then stopped.

"Oh, please, Cousin Skye - carry on with this; we play this one as a game at our junior school," Steven begged, stretching his body up from the couch to glue his eyes to the page.

"OK, then; as you're ready, I'll now begin," Skye reluctantly said, nonplussed by her cousin's option of rhyme, as the illustrator's shillings on the edge of the page brought home the pay she would lose.

She glanced at her cousin's naïve face before reading

the first two lines of the poem out loud, continuing after a pause until reaching the end.

"Thanks, Cousin Skye; that's my favourite rhyme in the book!" Steven gleefully cried, too young to perceive its reference to public beheadings and people in debt."

"If it used to be mine, it wouldn't be *now*," Skye begrudgingly thought, masking her angst with a smile as she rose from the couch and placed the book back on the shelf.

As she returned to the couch, both mothers entered the room, each carrying a platter of sandwiches cut into squares which they placed on the table next to the crisps.

"Hello, Skye," Mrs Hayes said, giving her cousin a hug. "It's lovely to see you again after such a long time. Are you just back from work?"

"Yes," said Skye, lowering her eyes; the question leaving her tense.

"Skye - is anything wrong? You seem a bit down," her mother enquired, eyeing her daughter with concern.

"No," Skye untruthfully said, reluctant to mention the loss of her job in front of her guests.

"Skye's probably just tired after work," compromised Mrs Hayes. "When one's new to a job, it takes time to adjust."

"Mum - I'm hungry; can we have our tea now?" Steven asked, jumping up from the couch to feast his large eyes on the food.

"We'll ask the host first," his mother replied, as Skye mutely stood by the hearth, reflecting on work.

"That's all right by me," her mother agreed, throwing her daughter another solicitous glance. "Skye can help me bring in the drinks - and then we can start. What drink would each of you like?" she asked her two guests.

"Can I have some cream soda?" asked Steven, licking his lips.

"Yes; I'll bring you some in," Skye's mother replied.

"A cup of tea would be nice," Mrs Hayes said, throwing the two hosts a smile.

"Then, if you and Steven both sit at the table, we'll be right back with the drinks," Skye's mother replied, as she and her daughter abandoned the lounge and entered the kitchen in haste.

"Are you *sure* everything's OK? You look rather subdued," she asked Skye, as she poured out the drinks.

"Yes," Skye tersely replied, having resolved not to tell her mother what was wrong until after their two guests had left.

"Is it work?" her mother surmised, as Skye switched on the kettle and laid out the saucers and cups.

"Not now, Mum; we have guests," murmured Skye, fetching two trays from the drawer.

Her mother resignedly sighed, placing the glasses filled with cream soda on one of the trays.

"I'll bring these drinks into the lounge," she despairingly said, causing her daughter to feel more uptight and distressed. "When you're ready, bring in the tea," she added, disappearing from the room with the tray of soft, fizzy drinks.

Skye poured out the tea, bringing it into the lounge on the tray that remained.

"Can we start?" Steven asked, sipping his drink.

"Once Cousin Skye has laid out the saucers and cups," said Mrs Hayes to her son, as Skye observed that the cake she had bought now sat out of its box, on a plate.

"It's OK, Steven; you can start; I'm about to sit down," Skye cut in, placing the empty tray by the couch before taking a seat.

Steven stretched out his arm; his hand closing in on a cup cake adorned with a bat made of edible beads.

"*Savouries* first," nagged his mother, placing a handful of crisps and two sausage rolls on his plate.

Skye passively watched as Steven rapidly hoovered the food from his plate, which he promptly refilled with cheese and pineapple sticks, and pate on bread.

"You're not eating, Skye," remarked Mrs Hayes, as both mothers helped themselves to a medley of bites.

"Skye - why aren't you having any food? Aren't you hungry?" her mother enquired; Skye's appetite quelled by the prospect of being unemployed.

"No," her daughter replied, harbouring her dread of breaking the news about losing her job once the two guests had left. "There was a function at work, and we had the food late."

"Oh, well - I suppose you'll be hungry in time, and will eat later on," said her mother, downing her last salty bite. "Anyone for a portion of cake?" she went on, addressing her guests.

"That's the cake that Cousin Skye brought home!" Steven piped up. "*I* want a piece."

"I'll have a piece, too," Mrs Hayes said, handing over his plate and her own to the host for a slice.

"Would *you* like a piece?" Skye's mother asked, cutting into the cake.

"I'll have a bit later on - with some savoury bites," her daughter replied, remembering the 'use by' date of the cake, which she hoped would not taste too stale.

Skye uneasily watched as her mother handed each guest a portion of cake before cutting a slice of the jammy, iced sponge for herself.

"Wow, Cousin Skye; it tastes out of this world!" Steven cried after taking a bite; leaving Skye relieved that the cake still tasted fresh.

"Good," Skye abstractedly said, remembering her vacuous purse. "At least it means that the cake has been money well spent."

The two mothers threw her a frown, perplexed as to

what she had meant, as she gazed at the face of the ghost that covered the cake to behold the eyes of her colleagues glowering back.

"Steven - finish your drink; we'd better make tracks. You've your homework to do - and then it will be time for your bed," said Mrs Hayes to her son as she glanced at her watch.

"Can I take some cake home?" Steven asked with wide, pleading eyes once he wolfed down his drink.

"Skye - would you bring me two plastic boxes and the roll of aluminium foil from the cupboard in the kitchen?" requested the host, slicing more off the cake. "I'll give you and Steven a lift," she added, addressing her guests, as her daughter abandoned the room to fetch the boxes and foil.

When Skye re-entered the lounge, her mother and cousins had on their coats, about to depart; each guest waiting to be handed their portion of cake.

"Thanks for reading me 'Oranges and Lemons,' Cousin Skye," Steven gratefully said. "'Here comes a candle to light you to bed, and here comes a chopper to chop off your head. Chip, chop, chip, chop. The last man's dead!'" he playfully sang, as his cousin packaged the slices of cake that her mother had cut.

"That's OK, Steven," said Skye, handing both boxes of cake to his mother in haste.

"Aren't you coming with us, Skye?" asked her mother, observing her daughter had not fetched her coat.

"I thought I'd stay here and clear everything away," replied Skye, wishing to spend the next half an hour alone.

"All right," her mother succumbed. "But be sure to eat something before going to bed. You look very pale - as if you've not eaten *anything* earlier today."

"OK," murmured Skye, reflecting that her mother had been right in sensing that she had skipped lunch.

"It's been lovely seeing you again; good luck with the job," Mrs Hayes said, approaching her cousin to give her a warm-hearted hug.

"Goodbye, Cousin Skye; thanks for bringing the cake," Steven squeaked, following suit.

"Goodbye; safe journey home; come again soon," Skye said to her guests, as they and her mother made their way to the door.

"See you later on - and make sure you eat," her mother advised, before all three relations abandoned the lounge to leave her in peace.

Covering the leftover bites, Skye heard Steven chant from the hall:

"'Two sticks and an apple say the bells of Whitechapel / Kettles and tongs say the bells of St John's—'" his infantile voice trailing off as the front door clicked shut.

Placing no food aside for herself on a plate, Skye set about clearing the table of leftover food, deciding to wait one more day before telling her mother that she had been axed from her job.

🕐 🕐 🕐 🕐 🕐

Two hours later, Skye lay in bed, waiting for the sleeping pill she had downed to kick in. She tried counting sheep - but all that would run through her mind was the nursery rhyme that her cousin adored, and believed had meant nothing but fun, sweetness and light.

"'Here comes a chopper to chop off your head,'" her thoughts relentlessly jabbed, reminding her of the job which - thanks to her colleagues - was soon to be lost.

Half an hour later, her eyes felt themselves close as the pill took effect, its paralysis merged with the dread of facing her colleagues the following day.

As her eyes slid open, she drifted downstairs, walking

out of the house past a church belonging to the past - before decimalisation was used. Slowing down, she looked to her right, where a stall was selling oranges, lemons and striped bullseye sweets as the church bells pealed buoyantly forth. Skye pulled half a crown from her pocket to pay for an orange, a lemon and eight ounces of sweets, only to find that the coin in her grasp did not cover the cost.

"You're five farthings short. You can pay me the difference next time you're here," the stallholder said, as she heedlessly placed the sweets and fruit in her bag.

Wearing a smile, she sauntered away, two tiles coming loose from the roof of the church as she browsed past a stall where fresh pancakes and fritters were sold, fried and tossed in a pan at each buyer's request by the stallholder's wife.

Skye walked on half a mile; yet only a minute had passed when she glanced at her watch. It felt as if she were gliding on air as she came to another outmoded street with a church and more stalls selling kettles, pokers and tongs. She looked down at two sticks and an apple that lay at her feet, next to three sixpenny coins that must have been dropped by a drunk passing by. She picked up the coins which she placed in her purse, deciding to pay the money she owed to the stallholder selling the bullseyes and fruit, when she made her way home.

She crossed the dank, cobbled road to head for a stall selling candles and choppers with razor sharp blades that looked indistinct in the mist; and as she drew close to the stall to examine its goods, the hideous loss of her job re-entered her mind.

Hearing footsteps behind, she looked round to catch sight of a priest emerge from the church, his figure growing increasingly close to the stall. As he came within inches of Skye, he drew to a halt; she and the clergyman now standing face to face in the autumnal mist.

"My name is Father Baldpate, Patron Saint of travellers and itinerants," said the priest, shaking her hand, as the stallholders mutely looked on - a man and a woman whose faces were shrouded by hoods. "You've lost your job, I understand," he added in a tone of regret. "But I'd like you to know that there'd always be room for you here in my church - if you became homeless, as well. Let me give you a piece of advice," he went on, as the mist gave way to a blanket of thick, swirling fog. "In future, never trust your colleagues; don't give them fuel for the fire by telling them too much. It would pay you to wear a false face; be more underhand, and let your future employer believe that you're happy in your job - even if you aren't."

Skye shrugged in narcotic fear, picking up a Gothic style candle from the stall as the priest disappeared.

"My cousin, Steven, would really like this," she said to the vendors of the stall.

"You owe us ten shillings," the stallholders said; their voices captious and cold.

"How *can* I - when I haven't bought the candle yet?" she quizzically asked, wondering why both their faces were still covered up.

The stallholders lifted their hoods; streams of dense, murky fog pouring forth from their mouths as the two of them laughed. Skye reeled back in shock; now she could see who they were: the male employer who pulled her to pieces, aborting her job, and the sly female colleague who gave him fuel for the fire by betraying her trust.

The woman started to grin; her eyes like daggers, pinned on Skye's face as she took out a wax taper match, which she struck, before lighting a candle that stood on the edge of the stall.

"By the way - here comes a candle to light you to bed!" she maliciously jibed, picking up the candle from the stand as the man seized an axe.

Karen Clark

Skye turned on her heels, fleeing in fear down the damp, foggy street in search of somewhere to hide from the danger she faced. Taking deep breaths, she paused and looked round to find herself being pursued; her employer and colleague close at her heels with the candle and axe in their grasps.

The fog increased as Skye continued to run, losing her footing on the kerb as her chasers caught up.

"Have you learnt your lesson now?" the colleague piped up with a pitiless shrug, as Skye lay flat on her back, frozen with fear.

"If you haven't by now, that would make you even thicker than I'd thought," her manager jeered as he lifted the axe.

The woman laughed, as Skye's P45 appeared in her grasp; her chortling growing increasingly shrill as the candle set it alight.

"And by the way," she callously screamed as the axe was about to descend, "Here comes a chopper to chop off your head. Chip, chop, chip, chop. The last man's—"

KEEP BRITAIN SANE

It was late November - the darkest time of the year, when leaves had abandoned the trees and the sun became mean, turning the climate to ice. Reign switched on her cellular phone, chewing her lip in defeat as she rushed through the blanket of foliage covering the ground. Her sister had bluntly rung off after bruising her ears with a stinging tirade - words which Reign felt were uncalled for and viciously cruel.

It was twenty past three, and the light was beginning to fade; the sun streaking crimson all over the sky before yielding to dusk. Hearing a rustling sound from behind, Reign stepped up her pace; and nervously grasping her phone, she started to run, frightened of being waylaid by "Keep Britain Sane" - cited the "KBS" by the public and press.

She continued to scamper as fast as she could; her pulse vibrating in fear. For Reign was mentally ill, but had so far managed to dodge the clutches of "Keep Britain Sane" - ever since the bigoted party came into being. The rustling still pounded her ears, but on nearing the end of the forest, she dared to look round; her body swamped by a wave of relief as a track-suited jogger sped past her to swiftly be lost.

Placing the phone in her bag, she made her way home, feeling uniquely at risk as her job would be lost; her workload had grown, and she felt unable to cope. As much as she tried to keep calm, she panicked when dealt out a task - and in the end she caved in, being left with no choice but to hand in her notice the previous day.

"What if the 'KBS' find out and set about hunting me down?" she thought, as she let herself into the flat that she shared with Janine - a carer, divorced from her husband, who only worked nights.

"Reign! I haven't seen you for weeks. How have you been?" Janine called, as she saw her flatmate come in.

Reign lowered her eyes; she was not in the mood to converse after such a hard week.

"Oh dear; you don't look too happy; is everything OK?" frowned Janine.

"No," Reign sorely replied, as her flatmate raked through the litter of post in the hall.

Janine seized two items of mail, turning to face her co-lodger in curious concern.

"It sounds pretty bad," the flatmate remarked, tucking the posted envelopes under her arm. "There's some time to go before my shift at the old people's home. If you want a shoulder to cry on, why don't we both have a chat in the lounge once I've made us a nice cup of tea?"

"All right," murmured Reign, not wanting to seem impolite; having hoped to spend the evening entirely alone.

"I'll bring these in with me for now to save going up to my room," Janine said, referring to the items of post tucked under her arm. "Come on; let's both go in," she perkily added, making her way to the lounge, as Reign followed suit.

Feeling fearful and tired, Reign made for the couch, while Janine bustled into the kitchen to make the hot drinks. During her wait, Reign switched the television on to divert her mind, reeling in utter disgust as she caught the tail end of the news. There on the screen lurked Dale Wolf - the menacing leader of "Keep Britain

Sane" - a man of about her own age, wiry and lean, with a handsome but mean-looking face; his eyes suggesting that he was not to be crossed. His members hung close to his side, listening in awe to all that he voiced, and keenly applauding his condemnation of those who were mentally ill. Each member was wearing a standard, four-piece, two-button suit in bright orange and green; their lapels adorned with the logo enacting their group: a Union Flag and reversed smiley mouth featured over a brain that was superimposed by a cross.

Reign switched off the set as Janine re-entered the lounge with a tray holding two cups of tea and a small slab of cake.

"I'll pop these things down on the table, and then we can talk," said Janine, ready to pour out the tea.

"I've packed in my job," Reign burst out, before Janine sat down.

Janine swiftly put down the tray, realising her flatmate felt plagued by the look in her eyes. She took a seat beside Reign; the plate of cake still in her grasp.

"When?" she curiously asked as she put down the plate.

"I handed my notice in yesterday morning - when I got in," Reign glumly replied.

"What led to *that*?" Janine asked with a look of concern.

"It all got too much - the workload, the people and everything else," Reign wearily sighed, letting her tea turn to ice as she stared at her cup. "I just couldn't cope in the end; it was driving me mad," she went on, feeling increasingly tense.

Janine picked up her cup, sipping her tea as she tried to comfort the flatmate that she hardly knew.

"Were you given too much work - or was it that you just couldn't cope with what you were given?" Janine carefully asked, sensing the raging fear Reign was trying to suppress.

"It was more subtle than that," Reign replied. "They made me do more than my fair share of work - but in only one field. There were other duties in my job description as well - but I'd panic, so they restricted me to the one task. There were snide comments from my colleagues regarding my 'inability to keep calm,' and the 'state of my mind.' The remarks built up - and so did the volume of work in the only area in which they thought I could cope. The atmosphere grew so bad in the end, that I felt I just couldn't stay. I suffer from anxiety, you see - and that makes things so hard."

"You don't have to tell me that," said the other, draining her cup. "I hardly know you, but from the moment I first saw you, I realised you'd suffered with nerves. People aren't always nice - and just by talking to you, I can tell you have a breaking point, if pushed a little too far."

Reign gulped with unease, somewhat taken aback at what her flatmate had said; she had not been aware that her breaking point rate had been so strikingly clear to everyone else.

"So I take it you haven't found another job yet?" Janine guessed by the troubled look on Reign's face.

"No," Reign tensely replied, "Nor will it be easy for me to do so - the way that I am. Why do you think that I still share a flat, pay a low rent and not live in a place of my own? I've dared not take out a mortgage and rely on whatever I could earn - in case I'd cave in on the job if the stress grew too much; either that or I wouldn't be wanted because of my nerves. The mortgage would only go bang; I'd lose the flat, and find myself out on the streets. Because of my nerves, I've experienced problems with jobs again and again - and it's ruining the quality of my life. My predicament was bad enough before - but the way society is now has made it much worse."

Janine put down her plate, and stared quizzically into Reign's eyes.

"What do you mean - 'the way society is now?'" she asked with a frown.

"The KBS - Keep Britain Sane," Reign sorely replied. They seem to have built up more power over the years - and are shown on the news quite a lot. They aim much of their bias at those who are anxious, nervous or mentally ill - people like *me*. Didn't you see their leader, Dale Wolf, threatening and laying down the law on the news the other night? What he was saying was really extreme."

"There's no way the KBS would come looking for you here - just for you giving up your job. No *other* party ever has - so why on earth would *they*?" Janine firmly replied.

"The KBS persecute people like me; they hunt certain citizens out," Reign said with a sigh.

"I doubt if it would ever come to them badgering *you*," Janine exclaimed. "But in the unlikely event that they *did*, and they came round here, I'd send them away; throw them off scent; pretend no one else was in, and say I didn't know who you were."

Reign did not reply; she threw her flatmate a smile, secretly sure that if Keep Britain Sane turned up at her door, Janine's loyal actions would fail to deter its members from entering the flat.

Years ago, when the movement began, the party was relatively tame; but over the years, its power had steadily increased; and had Reign given up on her job when the group had just formed, she would not have been as afraid as she was currently was.

Janine glanced at her watch, placing the half-eaten cake with her saucer and cup back on the tray.

"I must hurry up and get ready; my shift begins soon,"

she piped up, as Reign gulped down her icy cold tea. The care manager isn't exactly my most ardent fan; she doesn't need much of an excuse to try and trip me up; but I've learnt to look after myself," the care worker went on, hurriedly adding Reign's empty cup to the tray.

"Thanks for your words of support," said Reign, getting up from her seat, touched by what Janine had said about turning Keep Britain Sane away if they came to the door.

"That's perfectly OK," the other replied, as she picked up the tray. "Have a nice evening - and maybe I'll see you tomorrow," she added, heading for the kitchen to put away the cake and wash up the saucers and cups. "Oh, and by the way," she finally said, briefly turning back. "If the type of job you've been doing isn't working out, perhaps you'd do better trying some other kind of work."

🕐 🕐 🕐 🕐 🕐

The following morning Reign suffered a panic attack; her body an electric current of nerves as she dreaded facing the colleagues who made her feel small. About ten minutes later, the fit of anxiety passed, and she forced herself into the bathroom to wash and get dressed. On her way out, she realised Janine would be sleeping in the next room after her shift, and made sure not to make too much noise as she tiptoed downstairs. Entering the kitchen, she found herself loath to stomach even a thin slice of toast, and poured out a mug of hot tea, before forcing it down a tense throat that seemed to be blocked.

Within the next hour, she was sitting at her desk, deprived of tasks from the colleagues who blanked her as soon as she entered the room.

"Why don't you bring something in to occupy your

mind?" the telephonist asked. "You could read a book, or knit, or browse the internet on your PC."

"You can read *this*, if you like," the secretary joined in, slapping a newspaper onto Reign's desk with a smirk.

Reign opened the newspaper up and pretended to read the first page, wondering what sneering remark would be hurled at her next.

"What are you reading through *now*; looking for another job?" the secretary jibed, as she and the telephonist looked at each other and laughed.

The two women returned to their desks leaving Reign to stagnate in her seat without any work, riddled with guilt and unease as the telephonist glowered into her eyes to make her feel cowed.

When lunchtime arrived, Reign abandoned the office in haste, turning into a parade a few metres away. As she neared the town hall, a male voice enhanced by a loudhailer blasted her ears; but she was unable to see his face or decipher his words from a distance so great. She drew closer, to see a rally - held by a few politicians - take place in the street, as ardent supporters gathered around, brandishing banners with slogans in what they believed. At first, Reign plunged into denial, convincing herself that her eyes were deceiving her brain; but the fervour and din of the rally forced her to open her eyes and admit that what she observed was seriously real. An unpleasant sensation shot through her veins as she finally acknowledged who the politicians were, as their supporters swiftly flocked round, cheering at every sentence their leader yelled out.

Before her eyes - in the flesh - were the men she had seen on the news the previous day: the fanatical, bigoted members of Keep Britain Sane. Revolted and scared by the sight of these vicious, young men with polished facades, she stood in the crowd and looked on, appalled by their condemnation of those who were jobless and mentally ill:

the 'waste of space ciphers unfit to roam the free world which they ruined for those who were able to cope.' The whole theme of the rally resembled the mindset of those where she worked, who treated her as a minion because of her nerves.

Reign watched in disgust as the crowd waved their fists, shouting "Keep minorities and mad people out!" in one synchronous voice that baaed like that of a sheep; their banners daubed with the vile, evil logo of Keep Britain Sane: the flag, the cross, the brain and the miserable mouth that condemned the outnumbered, the poor and the mentally ill. Sick of the logo, Reign shifted her gaze to the zealots ahead, only to see the identical emblem on their lapels, as Dale Wolf's continuous rant bombarded her ears.

Then all of a sudden, the leader went quiet, moving the bullhorn away from his face which broke into a smile, as the crowd applauded and cheered, watching his henchmen submerge through the rear of the van used for their campaigns. Reign lingered ahead as the crowd dispersed to leave her standing alone in the midst of the square; the leader of Keep Britain Sane a mere metre away.

"If only he knew I hadn't been able to cope in my job - and what if he suddenly found out?" she fearfully thought, as she stood, waiting for him to get into the van.

But Dale Wolf remained where he was with the loudhailer clasped in his hand, as they stood, face to face; Reign struggling to hide her unease as his eyes met her own. For the first few seconds she felt relatively calm, as his manner suggested that he did not know who she was. Yet within the next moment, the look in his eyes became cross, raising her sense of alarm as she realised how clear it had been that she did not support "Keep Britain Sane" by not waving a banner or cheering along with the crowd.

She lowered her eyes, resisting the urge to hurry away

and make her fear and dislike look blatantly clear. She took out her phone and pretended to browse through 'overlooked' texts, subtly turning away from the merciless bully in orange and green. Slowly she retraced her steps; the back of her head perceiving his cold, probing eyes, as the garrulous din blaring forth from the politicians' van gradually waned.

After buying a sandwich for lunch, she continued to walk, greatly relieved that Dale Wolf was no longer in sight when reaching the street where she worked. As she entered the block, two colleagues walked out, stepping through the door with their heads in the air as if she did not exist, after which she ascended the stairs with a feeling of dread. Walking into the office, she found that her desk had been moved; now positioned close to the door - away from the rest of the staff. As she stared at the alteration in utter dismay, her supervisor approached, pointing at the newly-placed desk in a cavalier way.

"Don't worry," the supervisor smirked, "You'll find all your things are still in your drawer," and throwing her colleague a look to suggest that the problem was far from her own, waltzed back to her desk.

For the rest of the working day, no words between Reign and the rest of the staff were exchanged; and she struggled to bear the sting of their mutual sniggers and smirks until it was time to go home.

Once reaching her flat, she let herself into the hall, where she saw Janine at the foot of the stairs, dressed in her nightclothes and newly-awoken from sleep.

"I'm awaiting a letter," the flatmate announced, making her way to the stand to sort through the post.

"Oh, I see," Reign abstractedly sighed, frayed by the way her colleagues were acting at work.

"Reign - are you OK? You seem rather on edge," Janine said, looking up from the table in haste.

"While I was at lunch, my desk was moved near the door - apart from where all the other staff sat. Hardly anyone would speak to me either; and when I got up to go home, none of my colleagues said goodbye. I can't bear to go back and work my notice; but I need the money - and if I ring in sick, I'll go without pay, as I've no more sick pay to come," Reign sorely replied, removing her coat which she placed by Janine's on the stand.

"I wouldn't bother about what your colleagues do *now*. I know the atmosphere doesn't sound nice - but in a few weeks, they'll be out of your life - and you'll financially pick up if you find another job soon," Janine said, ceasing her search for the letter with a cool shrug.

"But that's just it; I don't think that I *will*. My nerves are too bad - and this job has taken away the little confidence I had," her flatmate replied.

Janine stared into Reign's eyes, before dropping her gaze.

"I suppose you could try signing on - but the Department of Employment doesn't take *everyone* these days; and if that doesn't work and you don't find another job soon, would that leave you with no other choice but to move out of *here*?" she carefully asked.

"Yes, it *would* - at least after a while," Reign replied with regret. "I only have a little money in reserve - which is going to run out - and the medical retirement pension I get is quite small; it wouldn't be enough to cover my rent as time would go on, and I'd plummet into the red."

"That would be a shame," Janine sadly remarked, securing the clips that held up her coarse, woolly hair. "I don't know you that well - but you seem so easy to get on with. *I* reckon you need to be bossier; to stick up for yourself a bit more - or others will be trampling on you for the rest of your life."

Reign lowered her eyes, slightly abashed, as she

realised that Janine was right; her colleagues had milked the fact that she suffered from nerves.

"Oh, and by the way," Reign declared; the memory making her tense, "I saw Dale Wolf and his cronies at lunchtime today - in the parade, near where I work; the KBS were holding a rally outside the town hall, where he was giving a speech."

Janine's eyebrows shot up in surprise.

"What? The KBS headquarters are in Keele, Newcastle-Under-Lyme - so I don't know what they're doing - coming all the way *here*," she incredulously cried, seeing by the pained look on Reign's face that her flatmate was telling the truth.

"The KBS are *everywhere* now. There will always be those who detest them; but their popularity and power has increased since they came into being - particularly over the past couple of years," Reign firmly replied.

Janine threw Reign a glance that was irked but slightly amused.

"OK - so the KBS are more prominent now than before; and I know I was shocked to hear that they'd come all the way to this neck of the woods when they hadn't before. But a general election *is* to be held very soon - and the KBS are not going to bother to focus on small fry like *us*. Besides, they don't even know who we are," she replied with a snort.

Reign mutely lowered her eyes. She deemed herself no more of note than the clapped-out, old man who lived two doors away. Nor had she felt that Keep Britain Sane had come all the way from Keele just to trail *her*; but Dale Wolf's dark glare when seeing her in the parade hours ago had left her unnerved.

The look of annoyance on Janine's pert face had remained, prompting her flatmate to end the discussion at once.

"Oh, look at the time; I must go. Have a nice evening," said Reign, as Janine made it tacitly clear she had lost her incentive to talk.

Reign made for the stairs, skulking up to her bedroom to take off her shoes.

As she massaged her sore, aching feet, the office's veto of trainers entered her mind, niggling and jabbing away until making her cringe. She reached for her slippers, which she slid on, shutting her eyes in dread at the prospect of having to bear her co-workers' spite, and seeing her notice through for another few weeks.

🕐 🕐 🕐 🕐 🕐

"Did you have a nice holiday, Chris?" the secretary asked, addressing the office accountant back from his leave.

"Yes, thank you; I *did*," Chris replied, as Reign sat at her isolated desk feeling wholly ignored.

"Listen, Chris - me and Jill are popping out to the shops; is there anything you want? We'll ask you more about your holiday when we get back." the secretary said, as she and the telephonist hastily rose from their desks.

"No thanks, Elaine," the accountant replied; his chubby face forming a grin as the two women put on their coats.

"OK then, Chris. See you when we get back," the secretary said, before she and her colleague submerged through the door to leave Reign and Chris in the office all on their own.

Reign felt her muscles contract, bracing herself for another instalment of hell, as she saw by the spite in her male colleague's eyes that he was about to home in.

"Oh, so your desk has finally been moved, then?" Chris wantonly sneered.

"*Finally?*" Reign bafflingly asked, not knowing what he meant.

"The other members of staff had been planning it for quite a while; it's just that they hadn't told *you*," he smugly replied.

Reign lowered her eyes; it was best not to rise to the bait.

"It hardly surprises me, though - as no one here's wanted to speak to you from the moment you joined," the accountant went on, eager for her to react.

Reign remained quiet; her face was deadpan, but her insides were cringing with shame.

"I noticed today that Jill and Elaine left you out again before going to the shops; they've been bad-mouthing you for a long time now - when you've been out of the room. I had to defend you three times before I went away - and that was in one afternoon."

"It hardly matters now, as in a few weeks I'll be gone," Reign finally replied, without sounding ruffled or cross.

"Oh, it will be the same *wherever* you go," Chris cruelly replied - a cutting remark which left her feeling unnerved.

Reign fell silent once more, but the bullying went tirelessly on.

"You know, it's funny," jibed Chris with a grin, "but the other day, I read in my local paper about someone like you. She hadn't been liked where she'd worked, and gave up her job without finding another elsewhere - exactly like you. The KBS found out about this - and once she'd signed on, they accosted her outside the benefit office for 'not being strong enough to cope'. They also found out her address, and harassed her with threats and abuse - calling her vile names online and in notes they pushed through her door. Graffiti was sprayed outside her house - and she received anonymous calls on her phone - branding her as 'mad and unfit to be in a world amongst those who could cope and were sane'. So if you've plans to sign on once you leave here, then I feel sorry for you. The KBS are now said to be hanging around benefit office grounds - badgering those on the dole; and there's nothing anyone can do, as they're growing in power. You may not have heard about this yet, but I expect that you will very soon. The only trouble is, though, you can't take back your notice, because no one's wanted you here, and your hand has been forced."

This was exactly the kind of nightmare Reign feared would play out; and as much as Chris had told her about it to fill her with fright, she sensed it was true, as Jill and Elaine returned from the shops; the accountant showing a friendlier face as he saw them emerge.

Reign spent the next several hours suffering alone, remaining completely ignored, as Chris, Jill and Elaine talked amongst themselves; and the staff who once gave her work evasively brushed past her desk, as if she were not in the room.

At five minutes past five, she sat, alone, on the bus. Seconds before the doors closed, Chris scrambled on board; his eyes throwing her daggers as he rushed past to hastily clamber his way to the storey above.

By half past five, Reign was home, relieved that Janine was nowhere in sight as she entered the hall and took off her coat, withdrawing into the lounge to gather her thoughts. She sat on the couch and closed her tired, aching eyes; the unopened letter she had plucked from the stand ensconced in her lap as she thought of the past several hours she had to endure. Now more than ever the thought of returning to work the following day filled her with dread. After what Chris had said about the unemployed woman being hounded by Keep Britain Sane, she knew that her mental ill health had been cruelly discussed.

116

Chris's vile, frightening words had also cast doubts on her plans to attempt to sign on: what if she were to exit the benefit office only to be stopped and mercilessly grilled by Keep Britain Sane?

Reign re-opened her eyes, pushing her doubts and fears to the back of her mind, as she studied the unopened letter that lay in her lap. Picking the envelope up, she unsealed it in haste, as she heard Janine's footsteps pervading the hall, hoping she would not decide to enter the lounge. Lifting out and unfolding the letter - sent by her sister, Shanelle, in Bexleyheath, Kent - she perused the first couple of lines, aware that the sender had no idea that she would soon exit her job.

"Dear Reign,"

the letter began.

"How are you? I hope you are well, that you've now settled into your flat, and that all's OK where you work. As for that hideous character, Chris - I hope that he leaves; but you know what they say: 'wherever you go, you always get one.' It's just part of life--."

Reign lay down the letter and sighed, aware that her sister's high self-esteem would prove her less of a target for ill-natured Chris. She picked up the letter again and continued to read.

"I'm writing to you to share my good news. I'm happy to say that I've just been promoted in my job, which I'll be celebrating with drinks after work at the end of this week. I'm now head of my auditing team, and am so looking forward to stepping into my ex-boss's shoes at the start of next week.

I'm sorry about the problems you've faced in your previous jobs. In fact, I wish that my employees were as honest and hardworking as you; you've just been unlucky, that's all. Perhaps the job you have now will bring you more luck, and will enable you to move into a flat which you won't have to share.

I know it's short notice, but I'm holding a party at my house this Saturday at 5.30pm to celebrate my 'increase in rank.' There'll be music, drinks and plenty of food. I know it's a long way for you to come, but I hope you'll be able to attend. It would be nice to see you again - and you can update me on how things are going in your job; so please let me know if you're able to make it as soon as you can - preferably by tomorrow afternoon. Mum will also be there, and so will my friends - so please come.

Anyway, Reign, take care - and I hope to hear from you soon.

Lots of love,
Shanelle."

Reign refolded the letter, stuffing it into her bag with a frustrated sigh. The last thing she needed right now was to go to a party of slick, prying guests, grilling her on a new job that had failed to work out. She took out her phone, resolving to turn down the invitation as soon as she could. Tensely, she started to dial; Janine waltzing into the room as she pressed the phone to her ear, in the hope that her sister would promptly answer the call.

A few seconds later, she heard Shanelle's voice; Janine submerging into the kitchen in haste.

"Hello, Reign," greeted Shanelle. "Thanks for getting back to me so soon. How are things?

"I can't come," her sister burst out.

"Why not?" Shanelle asked, her tone changing from friendly to frosty and cross.

"Something's come up," Reign replied, struggling to think on her feet.

"*What* has?" her sister indignantly asked, sounding as if she were just about to explode.

Reign thought of the first excuse that came into her head.

"I'm seeing a film with my flatmate on Saturday night," she uneasily said, preferring the sting of her sister's sharp tongue to a swarm of gossipy guests.

"And, I suppose a trip to the cinema with a flatmate comes before going to a party held by your own flesh and blood?" Shanelle sourly asked.

"It's not that *at all*," Reign replied in an effort to calm Shanelle down.

"Well what *else* could it be?" Shanelle snapped. "If my party were more important, you would have told your *flatmate* you weren't able to make it - not *me*."

Reign saw Shanelle's point, and discarding her impotent lie, came out with the truth.

"OK Shanelle," she began, wishing she had feigned the excuse that she had not been well. "If you're going to take offence, then I'll have to come clean. You wanted an update on how things were going at work, so I'm telling you *now*: quite frankly, they're *not*; I've had to hand in my notice, because the job just hasn't worked out."

Following a sigh from Shanelle, a silence ensued; and at first, Reign thought that her sister had ended the call.

"What happened *this* time?" Shanelle asked at last, considering the numerous jobs her sibling had lost.

"The usual," Reign ruefully said, "Because of my anxiety, they withdrew certain tasks, as they felt I'd panic and wouldn't be able to cope; and as soon as my probationary period was coming to an end, my hand was more or less forced. Hardly any of the staff will talk to me now, and my desk has been moved near the door - apart from everyone else's in the same room."

"So, it's happened *again*. I wonder what it is you're doing wrong to be treated like *this* all the time," Shanelle said, sighing again.

"I'm not doing *anything* wrong," Reign sorely replied, peeved that her confident sister had not understood. "I'm being treated like this because of my anxiety, that's all; and the benefit office won't give me disability pay, as according to them, I'm fit and able to work."

"That isn't good news," her sister remarked. "Do you think you'll still be able to pay your rent once you exit your job? If you *can't*, that'll mean you'll have to move out and live back at home."

"I could, perhaps, still pay the rent for a while," Reign replied, in the hope that sudden expenses would not arise. "But I may not find another job for some time; and even if I *am* allowed to sign on, I'd hate having to pay rent through the benefit office - not that my landlord may take tenants on the dole."

"Oh, Reign," soughed Shanelle. "How on earth do you manage to get yourself into such scrapes? I must admit, I wouldn't want to be in *your* position right now. But if you come to the party on Saturday night, no one need know that you're losing your job; we simply won't tell them, that's all."

Reign nibbled her lip. How could she really be sure that Shanelle would refrain from revealing the truth to her mother and friends before the party began?

"Look, Shanelle, I feel pretty dire, as things stand. I'll hardly be in the mood for a party on Saturday night," she regretfully said, deciding to stick to her foregoing plans, and shun Shanelle's party and friends. "And don't you agree that the fares to your house would prove costly for me at a time such as this - when I'm soon to be out of a job?"

"Mum and I will club together and cover your fares. It's too late to send you the money in advance - but you can have it when you come round," her sister cut in, determined that Reign would not turn her invitation down.

Reign sighed again. She knew how wilful her sister could be, regardless of how others felt.

"I wouldn't dream of you having to fork out; you're not responsible for *my* financial mess," she tried to persist, not only loath to be cowed by Shanelle's prying friends, but to be left feeling shamed by 'alms' from her family, to boot.

"It shouldn't prove much of a financial burden to *me*, now that I've landed a job with much higher pay!" Shanelle absurdly laughed, which left Reign feeling more riddled with shame than before.

"I'd still feel bad if you and Mum covered my fares; and the way I'm feeling right now won't make me good company for you, Mum or your friends," Reign flatly replied, peeved that Shanelle had not taken her chagrin on board.

"Oh, go on, Reign - come," persisted Shanelle. "Brooding alone in the flat will just make you feel worse. The party will help bring you out of yourself; help take the job off your mind."

Reign gave up the fight; there was no way Shanelle would give in, which left her with no other choice but to face her family and elder sister's friends on Saturday night.

"What time do I need to arrive?" Reign reluctantly asked.

"Six o' clock would be fine - but you could come a bit earlier on, if you like," Shanelle advised, relaxing her tone now that Reign had agreed to attend.

"OK then, Shanelle. I'll see you this Saturday evening

between five and six." Reign reluctantly said, wishing to end the call and to be left in peace.

"OK then; take care," her sister replied. "See you on Saturday, then. And remember," she glibly added before ringing off, "I won't breathe a word about your job to any of my friends."

Reign switched off her phone, placing it back in her bag, as Janine - still dressed in her nightclothes - re-entered the lounge.

"You don't look too pleased; is work getting you down?" Janine enquired, pausing beside the settee on which Reign glumly sat.

"Yes, it *is* - and to make matters worse, my sister's insisting I come to her party to celebrate her promotion to manager on Saturday night," Reign sorely replied.

"What's wrong with *that*?" Janine asked, throwing her flatmate a quizzical glance.

"I'm having a terrible time - seeing working my notice through," the other replied. "This morning I got into work to find that my desk had been moved near the door - far away from everybody else's in the room. Chris, the accountant, started to taunt me once getting me alone while the others were out - telling me that moving my desk had been planned for some time. He said that none of my colleagues had wanted to speak to me from the moment I started the job. As much as I need the money, I come home from that office feeling so bad that I can't bear the thought of going back there for even one day; and to be honest, I now feel I can't face anyone at all. I tried to explain all this to my sister just now, but she took offence; didn't understand how I felt. She's insisted I come to her party; and her friends will be there - giving me the third degree about the job that I'll lose. She's advised me to lie that I'm being kept on, saying she won't let them know that I'm leaving the job to become unemployed.

But not only won't I be in the mood for a party, but I fear she may split, and tell her friends what I've told her about my job on the quiet - before the party begins. And even if she *doesn't* spill the beans, maybe my mother - who she'll probably tell about it – *will*."

Janine abandoned her plan to exit the lounge, and took a seat beside Reign.

"Perhaps you should have lied to your sister, and said you weren't well," she remarked with a smile. "I've never met her - so haven't a clue what she's like; but if she's the type you can't trust, then you shouldn't come clean. There are times you need to be sly to cover yourself. Having told your sister the truth now means that you'll have to attend the party you'd hoped to avoid - so good luck with *that*! But once you turn up, just carry on as normal and pretend that everything's OK - even if you think that her friends may know that you're losing your job. Don't let them know that *you* know that your sister has split, whatever you do. By the way - where is the party being held?"

"At her house in Bexleyheath, Kent," her flatmate replied.

"That's a long way from here," said Janine. "Now you're also saddled with paying the fares!"

"When I told my sister I was losing my job, she said she and Mum would cover the cost."

"I hope she sticks to her word," Janine said, eyeing her flatmate in doubt.

"*I* hope so, too," agreed Reign. "I'm so worried about money, that I'm now going to *have* to try and apply to draw dole, after all - whether I get it or not." But you never know; it's worth a try, I suppose."

"If the Unemployment Department grant you dole, they'll make you seek work, and force you out to job interviews once you sign on. I still think it would be well worth you looking for some other kind of work; I can imagine the atmosphere in the office once you walk in," Janine remarked in a tone of regret. "But you must tell the benefit office you'd like to change your career; otherwise they'll keep sending you to interviews for the same kind of work that you currently do. Had you been me, I'd have abandoned that kind of work *ages* ago. There's no way I would have been kept - and you wouldn't see me go back. I've known a few people who've had office jobs - and they're bar workers now; they couldn't take the strain that the office environment involved. Do you think you'll go in again tomorrow? The atmosphere in your workplace sounds pretty dire."

Reign stared at Janine and sighed.

"Not as things stand. That Chris is the worst of the lot; and now that he's back from his break, he'll be giving me hell when we're together in the office alone. Yesterday, the atmosphere was worse than it's ever been before - and I wanted to run out," she sorely replied.

"Then you'll just have to ring in sick, and let all your colleagues clear up your work. For after all, from what you've told *me*, that's what they've been doing to *you*," Janine firmly remarked.

Reign looked down and sighed, recalling her dental appointment a few months ago. Jill was on leave, and Reign had asked Elaine for the afternoon off in order to attend the appointment at a quarter to three. Yet despite covering for Jill in her absence many times before, the manager summoned Reign into his room, scolding her harshly for 'planning to let down the team' by 'abandoning the crew while the office was one person short.' Reign clearly remembered him urging her to make appointments 'in her own time,' without bearing in mind that, come 5pm, both the office and dental practice concurrently closed. Whereas Jill would take days off work on a whim without being chastised; and indeed, a few hours ago, Elaine had granted her yet another day's leave; that day, of course, being tomorrow - when, by planning not to be in, Reign would be 'letting everyone down by leaving the office two members short.'

"Anyway - must make a move and prepare for my shift," Janine piped up, rising at once from the couch.

"Thanks for your advice," Reign gratefully said, as her flatmate made for the door, uttering "Take care," before disappearing upstairs.

Reign sat alone on the couch feeling anxious and drained, as she faced the awful dilemma of ringing in sick and being condemned, or going into work and being a target of spite.

🕐 🕐 🕐 🕐 🕐

Reign took a deep breath as she reached her sister's front door, having spent the whole journey to Kent reflecting that her absence from work over the past three days had made her fare harder to find.

Within seconds of pressing the bell, the patter of footsteps from the hall distracted her thoughts; her muscles growing taut as the door unlocked in one click, edging open to bare her mother's face from behind.

"Oh, Mum! You're early; I thought I'd be the first to arrive," she exclaimed in surprise.

"Come in, Reign," her mother replied in a standoffish tone.

Reign entered the hall and took off her coat, which her mother irascibly snatched whilst shutting the front door in haste.

"Mum - is anything wrong?" Reign uneasily asked, cowed by the irritated look in her mother's dark eyes.

"Come into the lounge. Shanelle and I are the only ones here - so its best that we talk before anyone arrives," said her mother, hanging Reign's coat on the stand.

Reign's unease increased as she followed her mother down the hall, realising at once that the anger she sensed had been linked to the loss of her job.

"Hello, Reign; would you care for a drink?" called Shanelle, as her mother and younger sister entered the lounge.

"No thanks; perhaps later on," Reign abstractedly said, bracing herself for a talk from her mother and Shanelle.

"Come and sit down," said her mother, taking a seat next to Shanelle on the settee.

Reign sat down on a chair in front of the table of food, facing her mother and sister in dread, as the latter parted her lips, ready to speak.

"Mum and I would like a quick word," Shanelle began, whilst she and her mother swapped looks. "It's about the money for your fares. For both Mum and myself, things have cropped up; we've both had unforeseen expenses to pay since I spoke to you last."

Reign stared at Shanelle in dismay; nothing but brazen aggression glowering back.

"So, you and Mum *can't* reimburse my fares, after all?" she assumed in despair, remembering how, a few days ago, Shanelle had promised that she would go halves on the cost.

"No, I'm afraid that we *can't*; and it wouldn't be fair on Shanelle if she covered the cost of your fare on her own," her mother cut in.

Reign longed to protest, cross that Shanelle had gone back on her word without taking her sister's predicament into account. Furthermore, if Shanelle could not be trusted to cover her fare, could she have lied about keeping the news that her sister's job would be lost from her colleagues and friends?

"I hear from Shanelle that you've handed in your notice at work," her mother went on, impatiently sighing before continuing to speak. "This seems to be following a pattern; you're failing to hold a job down. You can't keep asking for handouts from me and Shanelle. This may sound a bit harsh, but it's high time you learnt to stand on your own two feet."

Reign felt her heart sink, and looked to Shanelle for support.

"Mum has a point," her sister piped up, springing to her mother's defence. "And *you* were the one who chose to leave home - something there's no point in doing if you can't hold down a job and keep up with your rent."

Feeling frustrated and misunderstood, Reign nibbled her lip; the look in her relatives' eyes remaining incensed.

"Look - I tried; I honestly *did*," she strived to explain. "I'd always obeyed; I hadn't been sullen or rude; I'd never been late coming back from my lunch, and had always got into work each morning on time. Things turned a bit nasty, that's all."

"Well, that's life. People aren't *meant* to be nice; you're not going to change them - *wherever* you go; don't you realise that yet?" her mother sententiously replied.

"Yes," Reign sorely cut in, "But what you've failed to point out is that when one is anxious, people are *worse*. They sense your unease, and try to unnerve you all the more; and managers see you as a drawback rather than a help - depriving you of tasks that they give to the confident instead - even if they're thick - in case you'll panic and feel that you're not going to cope."

"Then confront them; stand up to them; try and prove them wrong. Just tell them: 'Look, I feel that you're passing me off as inept without having given me a chance; I *can* cope; give me the task and I'll *show* you I can," asserted Shanelle.

Reign felt even worse after her sister's dogmatic advice, since having realised within a few days of starting her job that the earliest signs of a worker no longer being wanted by a firm were not being allocated tasks that were linked to his job.

"They didn't want me, so they wouldn't train me up. There was definitely some bias towards me *somewhere* along the line, if they'd moved my desk all the way to the door. I can hardly point a gun to their heads and force them to keep me; what say do *I* have?" she said in retort.

Her mother stared at her closely and tightened her lips, as her misconceived daughter sat hunched on her solitary chair, bracing herself for yet more unwanted advice.

"OK, so you don't carry weight, and aren't good at your job; so you accept it and find a way round it. There's always *something* one finds hard to do; you're not the only one to have felt unsure of particular tasks. I've done, and so has Shanelle; various other people who I've worked with have, too. But *we've* all survived; still managed to hold down our jobs - as hard as we've found certain tasks. However, with *you* there have always been hurdles you've never jumped over in each job you've had. You must be doing something other people *aren't*. It's not only your work on which you are judged; there are other factors employers consider, as well," the older woman said in a resolute tone.

"Yes - and you must be careful what you say - because if you upset employers by rubbing them up the wrong way, they start to get awkward and then they close ranks; and we're both aware that you're not very tactful at times," cut in Shanelle; she and her mother exchanging looks once again. "You must be *particularly* careful when you're new to a job, as usually, whoever's first in is usually first out."

Reign's head felt excessively crammed. She could stomach no more of her relatives' meddling advice, which left her feeling dismissed and entirely misjudged - just like her colleagues had done - which increased her frustration that none of her jobs had worked out.

"Look - I haven't come all this way just to be nagged. I feel bad enough as it is without being chastised!" she peevishly snapped, getting up from her chair.

"The trouble with you is that you won't listen. No wonder your colleagues and manager have turned distant and cold. You can't go on like this for the rest of your life; you must settle *somewhere*; you're thirty-four years of age, for crying out loud," her mother affirmed.

A split second later, the doorbell rang out in the hall.

"This must be our first guest; I'll see who it is," Shanelle said, getting up from the couch and vanishing into the hall.

"I hope Shanelle hasn't told any of her friends that I'm losing my job," Reign anxiously said, aware that it was too late for her to flounce out.

"Neither I nor Shanelle can keep covering for you, Reign", warned her mother, tightening her lips, "And you can't keep moving back in with me when a job ends. I won't be here to pick up the pieces forever. I had you and Shanelle late in life. The house would have to be sold if I went into a home; haven't you thought about *that*?" she went on, as Reign retook her seat in despair, knowing that she and Shanelle were not close, and that the latter would not bestow her for long.

Reign and her mother abruptly looked round, as Shanelle and her closest friend, Jenny, waltzed into the lounge; Jenny staring at Reign in a penetrative way.

"Jenny knows," Reign miserably thought. Shanelle's told her I'm losing my job; now the whole world and his wife will probably know."

As Shanelle returned to her seat, Jenny pulled up a chair beside Reign, who realised that, sooner or later, the questions would start.

"Hello, Mrs Myers; it's nice to see you again," Jenny said to the older woman in a tone of respect.

"It's nice to see *you* again, too," Reign's mother replied. "Shanelle will get you a drink if you like."

"No thank you; I'm OK for now," Jenny said, turning her interest to Reign, whom she sought to address.

"Hello, Reign; it's lovely to meet you at last," she falsely began, swapping amused and clandestine looks with Shanelle.

"Hello," Reign flatly replied, evading her eye.

"I hear that you work for a life assurance firm in New Cross; have you been there long?" Jenny smarmily asked.

"No; I've been there five months," replied Reign, resolving to keep her answers as vague as she could.

"And how are you getting on there; do you like it?" Jenny enquired; Reign afraid that Shanelle and her mother were going to join in.

"It's OK," Reign tersely replied. "It's convenient for me, as the office is near where I live."

"You're sharing a flat at the moment, I hear," Jenny said, throwing Shanelle a sly glance.

"Yes. I live with a care assistant called Janine. We don't see much of each other, as she only works nights," answered Reign with a lackadaisical smile.

"I know what having to share a place can be like - so it's good that you don't get under one another's feet. But I expect that once you become established in your job, you'll buy your own place; bet you can't wait," Jenny said with a sceptical look in her eyes.

Reign promptly clammed up, realising Jenny knew perfectly well that the loss of a job forestalled one's chance of being able to purchase a flat.

"Excuse me, everyone," she murmured in haste, and rising from her chair, she hurried out of the lounge before Jenny could say any more.

Ascending the stairs in the hall, she hid in the bedroom that Marvin, her brother-in-law, shared with Shanelle; its walls neatly strewn with snaps of herself and her sister before they grew up. To study how they appeared in the photographs then, no difference in psychological health between the two girls could be seen; both looking as if they would sail through life without grief. Little did Reign or the family foresee that once she would reach the coming of age, anxiety would cruelly swoop down and rob her of the fulfilling life that she could have enjoyed.

Averting her eyes from her poised, former self, Reign sat down on the bed, dreading having to come home once her money ran out; to relive those nightmare days when her mother's neighbours and friends would visit the house and berate her for having no job - leaving her mother 'to cover the cost of the bills and council tax all by herself' - would prove too much to bear.

Her thoughts were disturbed by the patter of feet, as a voice invaded her ears from the passage beyond.

"Reign - are you coming down?" she heard Shanelle call.

But it was no use; Jenny's insensitive questions had rendered Reign loath to revisit the lounge and face Shanelle's guests.

"I have a bad migrane; I'm not feeling well," Reign announced through the door, regretting how much of her dwindling supply of cash had been wasted on fares.

"Can I come in?" she heard Shanelle ask.

Reign got up and walked to the door, pulling it open in dread, as Shanelle marched into the room, perusing her sister to see how poorly she looked.

"The migraine was hovering this morning, but now it's much worse," Reign hastily said, desperate to dodge the shame she would meet by encountering more guests.

"*That* was well-timed," Shanelle said in a sceptical

tone. "You were always like this when people came round - even as a child. If you're feeling *that* bad, at least wait until you feel better before travelling back home. It's getting late - so you may as well stay here tonight. Marvin will be back from work soon; I'll let him know you're staying overnight when he comes. In the meantime, I'll get you some painkillers while you stay up here and rest."

Reign could tell that Shanelle was not pleased as she exited the room, leaving her sister to cringe in lingering regret about wasting her fares. A few minutes later, Shanelle reappeared with a glass of water and two oval drugs in her grasp.

"Here, take these," she advised, placing the glass by the bed and the pills in Reign's hand. "If you feel better after a while, you can come down. Jenny's already asking where you are, and why you haven't reappeared."

"*Of course* Jenny's asking where I am; without me, she's no one to taunt," Reign bitterly thought as she swallowed the pills, realising that Jenny had known the truth about her job.

Moreover, the questions Jenny had asked were blatantly cruel; and Reign felt that Shanelle had been downright disloyal by complacently listening in silence; just looking on.

"And remember to try and come down if you possibly can," Shanelle advised.

"I'll see how I feel - and thanks for the drugs," Reign replied, as her sister abandoned the room and descended the stairs.

But no matter how long everyone waited, Reign never came down, remaining hidden upstairs for the rest of the night.

"So how did Shanelle's party go; was it better than you thought?" asked Janine, as she and Reign sat in the lounge of the flat that they shared.

"Not really," Reign glumly replied. "But I cut it all short by feigning a migraine and spending the evening upstairs. I stayed at Shanelle's overnight, as had I left then and there, it would have proved hard to get home at such a late hour."

"Oh dear," Janine remarked. "After the distance you'd travelled, and all that money that went on those fares! Did Shanelle and your mother cover the cost, in the end?"

"No," Reign ruefully sighed. "Shanelle said they both had expenses to pay, which suddenly arose - and my mother told me that she and Shanelle couldn't bail me out every time I was out of a job; she said I must learn to stand on my own two feet."

"So your sister *can't* be trusted, then," Janine dryly remarked. "And, has she spilt the beans to her friends that you're losing your job?"

"Looks like she *has*," Reign forlornly replied. "I could tell that her friend, Jenny, knew. Yesterday evening, Jenny was the first to arrive - and she was giving me the third degree; telling me that she bet I couldn't wait to be established in my job so I could get my own flat. I got the impression she was taunting me a bit, as there was a smirk on her face all the while."

"Did Shanelle and your mother twig you were feigning a migraine to shun further questions from guests?" Janine carefully asked.

"I reckon they did - because this morning, before I left Shanelle's house to go home, there was a bit of a row - when they accused me of hiding upstairs to avoid Shanelle's friends," Reign tiredly replied.

"Well, you *did*, didn't you?" Janine thoughtlessly quipped; a remark leaving Reign feeling hurt and misunderstood.

"Well, how would *you* like it if *your* sister split on *you* to a friend - and then sat on the fence whilst that friend taunted you with questions about what she should have kept to herself?" Reign defensively asked.

"I was *joking*," insisted Janine. "And, anyway, had I been you, I'd never have gone to the party and let things get so out of hand. You should have told Shanelle you felt ill last week when she rang; that way you wouldn't have wasted that money on your fares. Any trouble you sense, you must try and walk round; perhaps if you learnt to cover yourself more, you'd stop losing so many jobs."

"You're right, I suppose. What a mess I've got myself in; and my family don't seem to understand - which makes matters worse," Reign sadly replied.

"I can understand how frustrating their intolerance must be," said Janine, staring at Reign in concern. "But if you're going to live back with your mother - as you told me you might - you'll have to keep on both her and your sister's good side, and try not to argue too much. If I were you, I'd look for another job *now*, and try to hang on to this flat."

Reign nodded without a reply, aware that her latest job had destroyed the assurance she needed to impress a future employer.

"Will you be going into work tomorrow?" Janine carefully asked.

"Yes," Reign hesitantly said. "But I know the atmosphere will be dire - and I've no more paid sick leave to come.

"Do you have any *paid* leave to come?" her flatmate enquired.

"I've five leave days left, which I haven't had the chance to use up, as I've been too busy covering for everyone else."

"Well, you've only three weeks to go in that miserable hole; they can all just get on with it now; and as soon as you've gone, they can put on some other poor sod," Janine advised. "Take that week's leave, and contact the benefit office to try and draw dole."

⏰ ⏰ ⏰ ⏰ ⏰

Six weeks had passed, and Reign joined the queue in the benefit office, ready to sign on. She had been granted a jobseeker's handout, but not the disability allowance she had hoped to receive; the disability adviser having told her when she applied that no records of her illness existed on file, and that her anxiety did not exempt her from seeking a job. But his words had left her confused when she thought of how tasks in her previous job had been taken away due to Management's fear of her feeling too anxious to cope - a factor that finally led to the loss of her post.

She was third in line, and got out her card to sign on, as two women in the queue to her right began to converse.

"What happened to your job?" asked the first - a middle-aged woman in a checked, threadbare coat, with long, greying hair.

"It was OK at first," said the other, a youth who looked as if she were fresh out of school. "But after a while, they kept giving me more and more work - and it all got too much in the end, so I had to resign."

"How long have you been out of work?" the older woman asked.

"Only three weeks," the young girl replied. "But during that time, I've received nasty messages online - calling me a 'layabout,' and 'mentally unstable' for giving up my job; and saying that if I 'wasn't able to cope in the everyday world, then I shouldn't be in it amongst the sane, and those who could work'. I'm sure that the KBS have got hold of my password, home and e-mail address;

because that's what they're said to be doing to those out of work and the mentally ill - harassing them online; and when I got home one day last week, a note with the words "WASTE OF SPACE" scrawled across it was pushed through my door."

"I've heard about similar goings on," said the women in the coat. "The KBS are gaining more power and becoming a menace. I hope they don't trace my address and start targeting *me*."

"They've targeted quite a few of the mentally ill and those out of work," the young girl replied. "I hope I don't see them loitering outside on my way out of *here*."

"Then when we've both finished in here for the day, we'll meet at the entrance and both leave together; there's safety in numbers, they say," the older woman said, after which the two claimants fell quiet, as their turn to sign on at the booth finally arrived.

Reign felt her muscles tense up. She remembered what Chris had said about the unemployed woman being plagued by Keep Britain Sane, and the conversation between the two women in the queue had confirmed that what he had told her was definitely true.

During the next hour and a half, Reign's employment adviser scheduled an interview for her to attend the following week; and she spent the next thirty minutes pretending to browse the job-hunting machines, afraid of leaving the building in case a few members of Keep Britain Sane would be lurking outside. Then all of a sudden, Dale Wolf's ruthless face returned to her mind; the last thing she craved was to fall victim to him.

Wishing she were not alone, Reign took a deep breath before making her way to the exit and stepping outside. As she reached the rear of the building, her vision grew daubed with blurred figures in orange and green; and as what she saw see grew clear in her mind, she instinctively paused, ready to retrace her steps and exit the grounds the roundabout way. But the movement of torsos towards her caused her to freeze, as the flags, crosses, brains and reversed smiley mouths that defiled their lapels made it excruciatingly clear who her predators were. In the corner of her eye lurked the van used for their campaigns, obtrusively parked with the cars of the benefit staff where it did not belong.

Reign recognised some of these men from the news and the press; they were also in the parade near where she worked when Keep Britain Sane held their rally two months ago. But this time, Dale Wolf was nowhere in sight, which left her slightly relieved, though no less alarmed, as the men drew threateningly close before coming to a halt. Frozen with fright, she stood, face to face, with the deputy leader, Floyd Cole, warned by her instincts not to show fear as he parted his lips.

"We know where you live and your name - and why you abandoned your job," the deputy said, eyeing her in reproof, as if she had sinned.

Fearing that answering his questions would make matters worse, Reign took a pace back, trying in vain to avoid being waylaid.

"Let me pass. I've no time to talk," she evasively said, trying to sound as calm and firm as she could.

Floyd Cole and the rest of his men started to laugh; a tumultuous roar that echoed across the whole grounds.

"Had you been in a hurry to get off to work, you would have been believed; but being a lady of leisure means you have plenty of time on your hands," the vice leader said, whilst blocking her path.

"Even if I *do* have time on my hands, what's it to *you*?" Reign heard herself cry. "My struggles with work are between the Department of Employment and me; it has nothing to do with you and your party *at all*," she went on; her anger continuing to rise at being held up.

"You're obviously not too aware of the power our party has gained. If we win the general election next week, those without purpose like you would be taken in hand," Floyd Cole said, undeterred.

"Then you're going to be busy - because you should be aware by now of the thousands of people forced out of their jobs by predatory colleagues wantonly stitching them up; preying on the fact that they're anxious, nervous, weak, or mentally ill in some way. *They're* the ones to clamp down on - not people like *me*," Reign said with a snort, placing her hands on her hips.

"The people to whom you refer can hold onto a job. We don't care how obnoxious they are; they keep the economy going, and don't waste others' taxes on handouts to those who are of no use to the country *at all*," the deputy leader flatly replied.

It was a remark delivered 'straight from the horse's mouth,' freezing Reign into silence and turning her blood into ice. As the week had progressed, the events defacing her life had caused her to overlook the general election being held the following week: what if the nightmare of Keep Britain Sane taking charge of the country came true?

She resolved to stay quiet from now on, as Floyd Cole and the rest of his men carried on with their taunts; and two hours later, she reached the front door of her flat, nearly in tears, albeit relieved that the cruel persecution had stopped. But on entering the hall to sort through the post, she spotted a sheet of paper lying on the mat, and sensed it had not been delivered by the Royal Mail.

Reign hurriedly took off her coat which she hung on the stand, upturning the note after nervously picking it up. A note in the form of a poem scrawled in red ink - which could have been blood - caused her to reel, confirming her fears that she was now a target for Keep Britain Sane.

"WE WILL WIPE OUT THE WELFARE STATE,

AND WEAK INDIVIDUALS WITH NO INCENTIVE TO WORK, WHO WON'T PULL THEIR WEIGHT.

THIS WORLD IS ONLY A PLACE FOR THE FIT AND THE STRONG.

ALL YOU LOAFERS - GO BACK TO THE LAND OF INSANITY - WHERE YOU BELONG."

Entering the lounge, Reign switched on the laptop she shared with Janine, appalled to discover more virulent insults online; calling her 'a layabout,' 'thief,' and an 'indolent leech, feeding off the taxes of the rich and those willing to work.'

She started when hearing a rustling sound close to the door, fearing someone had forced their way into the flat to pursue the abuse. She looked round to catch sight of Janine hurrying into the room; the care assistant's expression bewildered and fraught.

"Someone rang while you were out," Janine announced.

"Who was *that*?" Reign curiously asked.

Janine massaged her head and looked down.

"I don't know," she tautly replied. "It was one of those anonymous calls where they shout down the phone; it wasn't very nice - and I wasn't sure if the call was intended for you or for me."

"What did they say?" Reign nervously asked, realising that it was *she* who the caller had meant to address.

"Well, as soon as I said 'hello,' they started to yell - calling me a 'parasite, living off the taxes that other people earned.' Then they shouted 'Waste of Space! You're a pariah who should be locked up, and kept apart from people who earn their right to be here.' I was also called a number of other vile names - those too vulgar to repeat. I wonder who it was. It may only have been someone mucking about - but it made me feel threatened and scared," Janine said in repulse.

Reign abandoned her seat, showing her flatmate the note she had found on the mat.

"This came through to door; I saw it when I came in," she confirmed in despair, as Janine studied the poem in utter dismay. "I've received an e-mail as well, similar to this - but I very much doubt if *you've* received one as well," she said, taking the note from her flatmate and folding it up.

"What makes you so sure that I *haven't?*" Janine edgily asked.

"I know who's behind this," Reign said with a feeling of shame.

"Who?" Janine queried, aghast.

"The KBS," replied Reign, pocketing the note. "I was stopped by some of its members outside the benefit office this morning - once signing on. They kept me for nearly an hour; bombarding me with taunts about giving up my job and sponging off the state. They told me they knew my name and address - so they must have got hold of my telephone number and e-mail address now, as well. I'm now frightened of signing on at the benefit office next time, in case they accost me again; and what if they win the election next week? *Then* where would I stand? I may have to live back with my mother sooner that I'd planned."

Janine shot her flatmate a glance of reproof, which took Reign aback.

"Yes - it looks like you *might* - and maybe you *should*," Janine fiercely replied. "*I'm* living here too, which means that if the KBS - or whoever the harasser may be - has a vendetta against *you*, then *I'll* be targeted as well. Every time I go out, I don't fancy the thought of coming back to threatening messages on the phone, or through the front door, or a brick through one of our windows - thanks very much. The longer you're here, the worse it will get; I wouldn't be able to live with that torment *at all*!" she frustratingly added, before flouncing out of the room and thudding upstairs.

Reign now felt entirely alone, resolving to ask her mother if she would take her back home. Her previous job and the bias of Keep Britain Sane were about to succeed in driving her out of the flat that she shared; the latter having destroyed her rapport with Janine. She took out the note, wondering whether or not she should call the police.

But first she would speak to the benefit office and urge its security staff to stop Keep Britain Sane from harassing its claimants once they signed on. She switched off the laptop and placed the note in her bag; and putting her coat back on, she exited the flat. A few minutes later, she boarded the bus, heading back to the benefit office where she had signed on.

Reign got off the bus and entered the building with care, heading for the entrance the long way around to avoid passing its rear, where Keep Britain Sane had waylaid her earlier on. When the security guard at the door asked her why she came back, she explained how Floyd Cole and his men had made her feel cowed; that they found out her name and address, and harassed her with phone calls, e-mails and unpleasant notes - all because she was out of a job, and claiming the tax payer's money that she did not earn.

She had hoped to speak to her appointed adviser about the harassment as well; but he was too busy interviewing claimants who had to sign on, which left her with no other choice but to exit the building and travel back home.

On her way out, she watched for anyone loitering

about who may hound her again, avoiding the rear of the building as she walked on. Nearing the exit of the grounds, Reign sighed in relief to see no one in sight; but a few seconds later, she froze in suspense as the Keep Britain Sane campaign van pulled up on the kerb; her heart leaping into her mouth as Floyd Cole and his gang of foul men emerged from its rear.

As they approached her, she turned on her heels, preparing to flee - only to find her path blocked as she had done before.

"So we cross paths again," Floyd Cole viciously sniped. "You love it here, don't you? You can't keep away. It's clear you've no intention of finding a job," he coldly went on, as he and his followers threateningly gathered around.

Reign took out her phone from her bag.

"If you're not careful, I'll ring the benefit office and get the security guard to come to my aid. I've already reported you to him - minutes ago," she angrily warned, preparing to dial.

"I wouldn't do that if I were you," the deputy leader advised. "When we win the election next week, the benefit office will have no power to do anything *at all*; Keep Britain Sane will ensure that it does not exist."

"You haven't won *yet*," Reign said in retort, cross at having been baited a second time round.

"I wouldn't keep riling me if I were you. Our party is racing ahead in the poles. More branches have opened up in our name since we joined the political race - or aren't you aware? People in your position are standing on seriously dangerous ground - particularly now that we're on the verge of being in power. You're not the first to be stopped and targeted by us. But the time has come to start taking things to a more mature stage," he resolutely added, as two of his members homed in, seizing Reign by the arms.

"Where are you taking me?" she yelled, trying in vain to break free.

"To our new branch," Floyd Cole flatly replied, as she felt her body and legs begin to advance.

All of a sudden, she found herself trapped in the back of the van; sitting among the members of Keep Britain Sane, as the driver sped down the road, leaving the grounds of the benefit office behind. She glanced at her watch to note it was only a matter of minutes before the van turned a corner and swiftly slowed down. In seconds the vehicle pulled up, after which she was ushered out of its rear and on to the street, looking toward a gated building of multiple floors. The men led her inside, and then down a passage with posters in orange and green daubed on its walls, each flaunting the prejudiced logo of Keep Britain Sane.

The members ground to a halt, once reaching a door besmirched with fly-posters of Union Flags and far right-wing slogans condemning abortions, help for the jobless and socialist views. The billboards resembled a brain smeared with the phrase: *"Debar the mentally ill,"* leaving Reign feeling sick, as Floyd Cole clenched his bigoted fist and rapped on the door. Within seconds, a voice she had heard on the media before uttered "Come in," after which Floyd Cole thrust open the door, revealing the face of the person to whom it belonged.

The nightmare Reign feared had come true - as there, at his desk, centimetres away - sat the member of Keep Britain Sane who scared her the most: the leader, Dale Wolf, whose cold, leaden eyes had pierced her like bullets in the square nearly two months ago. With a glacial nod, he signalled her to sit down, and she took a seat at the opposite side of the desk. On the wall that she faced, a fixed screen with the volume turned down captured her eyes, airing scenes of 'fortification groups' called

'Sentinels,' formed on behalf of Keep Britain Sane. They comprised gangs of young men armed with chains and iron bars, guarding the party's marches and rallies from left-wing dissent: an example of how inauspicious the movement could be. Having seen these groups wielding these improvised weapons on her television many times before left her horribly aware of why these marches took place in areas where unemployment was high and dwellers were desperately poor: to launch propaganda by battling with counter-protesters who they could seek to politically exploit.

Reign shifted her eyes to the desk, where at Dale Wolf's side sat two neo-fascist magazines - both produced and revised every month by the leader himself. One was entitled "Ignite" - aimed at students and youths, and circulated in colleges and schools; inciting learners to form activist groups and musical bands in order to drive ethnics, the poor, the weak, the mentally ill and anti-nationalists away. The other periodical, "Crusade," was placed on the shelves for the older Keep Britain Sane supporter to buy - used to voice the party's dislike of the welfare state, social justice and other socialist views.

Reign could no longer bear her unease, as the seconds of silence built up.

"Where am I, and why am I here?" she heard herself ask; a surfacing anger abruptly outweighing her fear.

"You're in our sub-office," the leader replied. "Keep Britain Sane has just opened it up - and I think you know why you're here," he added, as if she had broken the law.

"Is this because I've signed on?" Reign surmised, remembering the party had left her alone when she worked.

"Yes," the leader replied, keeping his eyes firmly fixed on her own to make her feel cowed.

"Could you elaborate on that? What, exactly, is it

about me drawing the dole that's causing you offence?" she almost snapped back, as her anger increased.

"You must be aware of the general election that takes place next week. We are tipped to win in the poles; you wouldn't be claiming benefits under our rule," the leader affirmed.

Reign let out a frustrated sigh, remembering how those with whom she had previously worked had exploited her weakness and forced her to leave.

"Who *would* your party grant benefits to, then?" she enquired, refusing to hide her objection to what he had said.

"They'd be granted to none but the basic, the very young, the very old, the sick, the severe and the obviously disabled - an umbrella that doesn't include those such as yourself. Keep Britain Sane would abolish the welfare state as it's currently known - which discourages civilians from marrying - as it's done *you*. The benefits system also heavily supports single parents. Our party is no supporter of feminist views. We believe that the single woman - particularly those like yourself, who is unable to keep cool under pressure, and finds the onus of a job too much to bear - should make way for the woman who is more psychologically sound, and able to cope. You are wasting the state and taxpayers' hard-earned cash by claiming handouts you hope to be scrounging for the rest of your working life - because you know that any kind of employment you happen to find would not probably last. Keep Britain Sane won't support you; we feel that women like you have a duty to cease congesting the welfare state by becoming a twenty-four-hour mother and wife."

Reign's anger grew more intense, as she felt the urge to abandon her seat and start kicking the desk. Dale Wolf's despicable words had rekindled the miserable days of her youth when she was constantly nagged for not being in a bond with a male - a step towards wedlock to steer her out of the province of work. Then all of a sudden, the latent volcano within her began to erupt.

"I was attacked by a male - attacked before I was old enough to start going on dates!" she heard herself cry; her voice increasing in volume with each word she yelled. "Once you're attacked by a male, you can't simply shrug, pick yourself up, dust yourself down, and get on with life; that's not the way that it works. Once you're attacked, not only are you scared it will happen again - but it alters your view of the way you see others as well as yourself. Since being attacked, I've been scared of living with a man, because I've feared he may end up knocking me around. Why in the name of the Lord can't anyone see that? Why are you people so thick?"

On the screen in front of Reign's eyes, an activist from the far left was viciously struck on the head by a Sentinel with an iron bar, as the leader's hard face masked his shock at the outburst she hurled.

"Then it's simply a case of choosing to bend or to starve," he nonetheless said, refusing to take Reign's excuse for having stayed single into account. "We've all known, if not heard, of female victims of attack who have married and managed to settle down in the end. They've seen sense not to carry on begrudging men for the rest of their lives; as by doing that, they only work against themselves; they never move on and progress - as *you* haven't done."

Reign mutely lowered her eyes. As grossly unfair as she found what Dale Wolf had just said, she resolved not to try and hit her point home, for fear he may deem her more mentally ill than she was.

The injured rebel on the screen who the Sentinel struck was carried away on a stretcher by the police, as the fray between Keep Britain Sane and the counter-protesters pursued.

"You've no hope of hiding behind benefits for the rest of your life - so get that goal out of your head," the leader resumed. "As you're no doubt aware, the Labour Party is currently in power, and plan to reintroduce the Incapacity Benefit that the Conservative Party phased out a decade ago, and which the latter replaced with less generous handouts for those who were plainly no use to society at all: the incapable and the insane. Keep Britain Sane will go one stage further than that in its effort to quell the five giant evils of society contained in the Beverage Report of 1942: squalor, ignorance, want, idleness and disease," he hard-headedly added, as on the screen, the conflict between the opposing two factions increased. "We will also gradually erase state pensions by rising the retirement age - a scheme that the Labour Party had planned to repeal. The number of qualifying years of National Insurance required to draw the pension will also increase - before we abolish it for good. The days of women retiring at sixty are gone and shall never return. By implementing the above and confining the Welfare State to the few who clearly can't cope, we will save the economy of this country billions of pounds. We will imbue into the young from the moment they're born that nothing beneficial is achieved without work, discipline and strife."

Reign let out a scurrilous snort.

"Now *there's* an ideal; one that in practice just wouldn't work!" she remarked, forgetting her nerves and what had occurred on the screen.

"Those who are disinclined to work will always say that," the leader replied, perceiving that Reign had loathed every job she had held.

"Your political party has no idea of what the world of everyday work's really like," she said in retort, recalling how she had been dealt more than her fair share of tasks in the past. "There are employees who are praised for having done no work *at all*. These so-called 'hard workers' form into a clique - and then do whatever they please: come into work late; take too long for lunch; go on holiday whenever they choose. They put on some poor individual to cover – to do all their work - while they're skiving and swanning around; and their manager turns a blind eye; won't get involved; couldn't care less - as long as the work is got out. There'll always be staff like that who keep jobs and will work their way round sharing any of the workload at all; and it's the vulnerable workers like me who they dump their work on. And in case you haven't yet sussed, these bullying cliques target those in the workplace who are anxious, like me - who they scare, taunt, put all the pressure on, and end up driving out. But you bunch of glorified fascists can't see the wood for the trees; you're too busy ensconced in a fantasy world of your own to be able to see what's really going on!"

All of a sudden, the fighting between the two factions came to a head, forcing Reign's eyes and attention back on the screen. She watched in dismay, as a left-wing counter-protester was killed in cold blood by a support group member as he tried, in vain, to intervene: a despicable scene to suggest that the former was axed from the world on behalf of Keep Britain Sane.

Dale Wolf had replied to Reign's view on workers and cliques; but Reign had not absorbed one word of his blinkered remarks, as the hideous gore that spewed forth from the screen threw her mind.

"Look what your party has done!" she cried in disgust, pointing to the screen. "Your demonstration has led to that activist's death! Those pre-election votes must be rigged. How could the majority of citizens want you in power? You're nothing but a bunch of bigots and legalised thugs!"

The colour of the leader's cruel face changed from white to deep red, and pressing a switch on the wall by his side, the screen promptly went dead.

"That's enough!" he furiously yelled. "Do not forget where you are, and that you're detained! When you first walked into this room, you asked me why you were here - and I'll tell you why *now*," he went on; his tone remaining irate but less fierce than before. "We brought you here to radicalise you - to mould your mind into ours. But it's clear to me now that you're simply a case beyond hope; one that our party would never be able to convert: blinkered, stubborn, self-centred, idle, tenacious, negative, self-defeating, unwilling, feckless, anti-male, totally left-wing, and a burden to the economy and society as a whole. Your uncooperative manner has already played a part in ruining the quality of your life; but it is clear that under our rule, you won't even survive. Our party need take no steps to reprimand you. All we need do - as you're no good to us - is simply to leave you to struggle in the new society we'll create without any aid or subsistence at all. So even though you're a disgrace to humanity by not having raised a family of your own, as well as having proved yourself unfit to hold down a job, I've decided to release you from here. When we win the election in a matter of days, and are in unlimited control, you'll find that you won't be wanted by society *at all*. You will be constantly looking over your shoulder for opposition from our Sentinels and groups, and for graffiti to be randomly sprayed across your front door; and as you've experienced already," he coldly went on, referring to the odious note that was pushed through her door, "the hostility towards you has already begun to take hold."

"So, those messages telling me to 'go back to the land of the insane' via phone, e-mail and note - they were from *you*," Reign wearily sighed, eyeing Dale Wolf in reproach.

"They were messages targeted at you on my behalf. We keep a database of those who've signed on. We've also the names and addresses of our opponents on file, which enables us to defend ourselves from potential attacks," the leader confirmed.

"I'm not a member of any of your opposition groups. I'm not a Zionist, anti-fascist, communist, trade unionist, or anything else," Reign replied, feeling unfairly harassed. "I'm hardly likely to lie in wait outside a town hall during one of your meetings with an axe - so there's no need to home in on *me*. And look at the damage you've caused by sending those threats to my flat? Because you've targeted *me*, my flatmate's now scared, as she feels that in turn, you'll start terrorizing *her*. She's turned hostile towards me since having been on the receiving end of a call from Keep Britain Sane while I was out - labelling her all sorts of vile, antipathetic names that were intended for *me* - not *her*. She's an innocent party in all this; she holds down a job, and has never signed on in her life. Do you honestly believe that *she* should suffer, as well - even though she's not on the list of the people you hate? And because she's scared of the flat being targeted by you, she's now saying that I should move out - as the longer I'm there, the more frequent the harassment will get. Please - for her sake - would you be willing to stop all the threatening calls and notes to my flat?" Reign imploringly asked, dreading the thought of having to find a new home.

The leader's impassive expression stayed wholly the same, as Reign fought to contain her panic at having felt trapped in a corner from which she could not escape.

"You know our answer to this," he coldly replied. "Until either you manage to prove you can hold down a job, or you marry, breed children and settle down - which would leave the responsibility for your keep entirely to your spouse - the e-mails, phone calls and notes of abuse will not stop. Keep Britain Sane won't change their policies just to suit *you*," he firmly went on, throwing her a look to suggest he had nothing to add.

He pressed the switch on the wall, and the screen displaying the clash between left and right-wing supporters sprang back to life; and as much as Reign loathed all the chaos and bloodshed it caused, now more than ever, she grasped the left-wingers' protest.

"I trust you know your way out," he said, in a tone to suggest he had found her no use to his ultra-right group. "And I'm giving you this, in case you don't know your way home," he added, handing her a map to show where his sub-office was in relation to her flat.

A few minutes later, she left the building dumfounded and frozen with fear; the Union Flag by the entrance stinging her eyes as she thought of the days ahead and her torment to come.

🕐 🕐 🕐 🕐 🕐

It was Thursday, 6.30am - the day before the result of the general election would be announced. Reign stood in the queue, ripping to shreds another inimical note scrawled in red ink, as she waited in line for the polling place to wake up.

At 7am, the queue came to life as the building unbolted its doors. Reign got out her poll card in haste, which she was ready to hand to a member of staff in exchange for a sheet containing the MP's and parties for which she could vote. As the queue edged forward, she studied the voters in front; their faces wholly deadpan and revealing no clues about which political party they wanted to win. Some were frightfully old - citizens Keep Britain Sane would deem fully inept for the resolute world they intended to build. But the bulk of these voters seemed sanguine and fit; probably those with good, steady jobs who were likely to vote for a party like Keep Britain Sane; an action they would regret if they were to fall ill or infirm, and required help from the state.

As Reign reached the entrance, she handed her card to the poll clerk who gave her a ballot for casting her vote. Once reaching her allocated booth, she studied the list of MP's and the relevant parties contained on the sheet; her eyes and nib evading Floyd Cole of Keep Britain Sane.

Hoping the current political party would rule for another five years, her eyes scrolled down the list; her fingers marking a cross by her Labour MP. After slipping her ballot sheet into the box, she made her way home, scared of the prospect of Keep Britain Sane seizing power within the next twenty-four hours, since being warned by Dale Wolf about what her life would be like if his party prevailed.

Once reaching her flat, she took off her coat; and recalling Janine would be spending the next few days with her boyfriend in Wales, she entered the lounge, deciding to stay up all night to watch the results.

Early the next morning, she woke up to find her body still slumped on the couch. As scared as she had been the previous day of Dale Wolf and his bigoted party winning the race, she had felt sorely tired, and had slept through part of the voting the previous night. The television screen - active and bustling with noise from yesterday evening - replenished her mind, waking her up to the fact that the day she had feared for a very long time had finally arrived.

With comatose eyes, she peered at the screen, and wondered if the laborious voting had stopped, recalling that only last night, Keep Britain Sane were still ahead in the poles. But in seconds, Buckingham Palace appeared on the set, and she knew that the final result had already come in. Scared of the outcome, she muted the sound and averted her eyes from the screen, giving herself a short while to gather her nerve.

A few minutes later, she turned up the sound, and forced her eyes back on the screen; and as Downing Street suddenly appeared, she took a deep breath, expecting to see Dale Wolf's face outside Number Ten. Then the famous door opened, and amidst all the clapping and cheers pouring forth from the set, the Prime Minister and his loyal wife promptly emerged.

With a squeak of surprise, Reign heard the elected leader deliver his speech, as he laid out his political plans for the coming five years: prescription fees to be scrapped; Incapacity Benefit and nationalisation to be reintroduced; European Union nationals to reclaim the right to remain; free personal help for the old needing help with day-to-day tasks; care and support for the mentally and physically ill; the national health service and welfare state to be given a boost; the minimum wage to be raised; state pension hikes to be stopped. These were the plans she had hoped for but thought would be lost; schemes that a right-wing party would never endorse.

"What a turn-up for the books!" she heard herself cry, recalling the bias she had met since having signed on; whilst being glad that, at the last minute, the public saw sense.

The Prime Minister wound down his speech, returning his pipe to his mouth with a jubilant smile, before he and his wife re-entered the home where they would reside for at least another five years. The Cabinet trailed them inside, each member's rosette not orange and green, but Labourite red; no Union Flag, brain or reversed smiley mouth adorned on each suit; just a friendly red rose.

Reign felt her anxiety wane, convinced by the final results that for all the political might Dale Wolf's party possessed, the country would never be governed by Keep Britain Sane; its beliefs being far too extreme, old fashioned and harsh for a nation to bear.

And yes - perhaps all the hype; the far rightist marches with Sentinels brandishing weapons to overawe counter-protesters and underprivileged beings; the hounding of benefit claimants, the mentally ill and minority groups, and the beleaguering phone calls, e-mails and notes would always remain; and Reign would always still suffer bouts of unemployment through the bias and cruelty of managers and co-workers alike. But now all these nightmares had veered to the back of her mind, as she knew that Labour was not going to hound her, force her to marry or take her benefits away.

Pressing the remote control, she switched off the set, before going out into the hall and donning her coat. Without looking over her shoulder, she exited the flat to go for a walk; and stepping into the street, remained pleasantly shocked that the Labour Party had won. She would sign on again next week without being afraid; and if on her way out of the benefit office, members of Keep Britain Sane waylaid her again, she would tell them their party had lost the electoral race, and were therefore in no position to cow and dictate.

THE TWENTY-THIRD
CENTURY WORKHOUSE

E ve crossed the main road; her arms aching and sore from the case in her grasp. Less than forty-eight hours ago, her mistress had plied her with praise for her loyalty and tact, as well as her excellent work; but now she was out on the streets with nowhere to go. It was hardly her fault; her night bus came late, and she a made it back to the house merely five minutes past the limit her curfew allowed. But as much as she tried to explain to her mistress that she had not been to blame, the excuse simply fell on deaf ears; and as Eve had witnessed quite a few times, one careless, inaccurate move meant a serf would be out.

As she reached the job agency entrance, she lay down her case, which was crammed with belongings and clothes amassed over the years. Now that her hands were untied, she took her character reference out of her bag before placing it in the pouch at the side of her case, ready to show to the first recruiter who happened to be free. She spent the next sixty seconds taking her handkerchief out to wipe the tears from her face; not tears of grief, but of doubt amidst the shock of losing her previous job as well as her home.

Having gathered her nerve as best as she could, Eve picked up her case, and taking a fathomless breath, pushed open the door to enter an office with time sheets and multiple desks. On the walls hung sepia-toned snaps of servants shot during the days before Britain's Master and Servant Act of 1923 was repealed, only for the act to be reintroduced in 2322. Eve observed the black gowns, white aprons and caps worn by the maids and the plain, dark-coloured waistcoats, cravats and white shirts the man servants wore during those far off eighteenth to early twentieth century years.

But since the Master and Servant Act had returned, certain roles and the dress codes of servants had drastically changed. Coachmen, stable boys and grooms were no longer required, as the car had long since replaced horse-driven carts. Dairy maids, too, were no longer required, as in this day and age, superstores sold all the dairy products one craved. The laundry maid had been replaced by the help, who exclusively ironed, thanks to the launch of the household washing machine a few centuries ago. The nursery maid's role was also extinct, the nanny now in sole charge of helping her mistress to cope with her children's domestic affairs.

Although sculleries still existed in certain abodes, the scullery maid's role did not. The only servants to remain were the cleaner (or housemaid as it used to be called), the cook, the housekeeper (who was the principal servant, responsible for the orderly running of the house), the valet, whose role involved tending to his master's needs, the lady's maid (the female coequal of the valet, who tended to her mistress and nobody else), the cook's help, who performed simple tasks, set the table before meals and forever washed up, the gardener (if the home had a garden), the casual staff - the only employees who did not reside in the house - and the nursemaid or nanny, if one was required.

"Would you come this way, please?" called the recruiter, who sat at the end of the room.

Eve sidled her way down the gangway of desks, struggling to hold in her fear of spending the night on the streets if not finding another position within several hours.

"What post are you seeking?" The recruiter enquired, as Eve took a seat at the desk, taking the character reference out of from her case.

"This is the character reference from my previous employer. I'm seeking a similar post to the one I had before," she said, handing him the note which he took and briefly read through.

The recruiter finished perusing the letter and focussed his eyes back on Eve.

"That's quite a good reference I see," he remarked, looking somewhat bemused. "But I take it you've already left the post," he added, seeing by her overfull case that she was between jobs.

"I left it earlier this morning," Eve said; her mind too exhausted to steer her from telling the truth. "As you can see by my reference, I was diligent and polite at all times - totally able to meet all my mistress's needs. The only problem I met was arriving back at her house a few minutes past the midnight curfew early this morning; the night bus was late to arrive. I was taken aback when she didn't accept my excuse, and asked me to leave."

"An expensive mistake to have made," the recruiter remarked, offering no words of support. "However, there *is* one lady's maid vacancy waiting to be filled," he routinely went on, browsing the available post on his computer screen. "The mistress is a widow, and in sole charge of the house. It's not far from here - "Harpenden Road" - a few streets away, so you wouldn't be lugging your suitcase too far if you went. Are you interested in the vacancy, at all?"

Eve sat up in her seat, feeling a glimmer of hope.

"When are the interviews held?" she hastily asked, desperate to shun a formidable night on the streets.

"I'll ring the employer right now, and see if she can see you within the next hour," the recruiter announced, keen to have the vacancy filled straight away.

"Thank you," Eve passively said, knowing she had no choice but to try for the post.

The recruiter picked up the receiver and started to dial, reaching the other end of the line straight away.

"Hello - Mrs Hart?" Eve heard him pipe up. "I have someone here for the lady's maid post; she can start straight away."

"During the minutes that followed, the recruiter blushed with unease; his tongue coercively stilled by the woman he rang.

"Well, it's up to *you*, Mrs Hart," he finally said, sounding repressively cross. "And you *did* say you needed the vacancy filled right away; so do you want me to arrange an interview with this lady, or not?"

The recruiter fell silent again, as he listened to what the lady of the house had to say; and within the next minute, the call had come to an end.

"Mrs Hart has agreed to interview you in an hour," he routinely announced, plucking a form and pen out of his drawer. "In the meantime, you can fill in this form and register with us," he went on, handing Eve the sheet of paper and pen. "Mrs Hart will ring you with her decision by late afternoon - so remember to keep your phone switched on for her call."

After a nod of accord, Eve spent the next fifteen minutes completing the form, after which she thanked the recruiter and left the agency in haste, deciding to make her way early to "Harpenden Road."

Eve reached "Harpenden Road" to find that the house looked quite big, although not as large as the one where she previously worked. She spent the following few minutes poised by the gate, observing its latticed bay windows and pebble-dashed walls. Whilst trying to decide whether or not she should wait until the set time before ringing the bell, a middle-aged woman with no chin and a hard, sour face abruptly brushed past her to bustle her way down the path that led to the porch. The woman took out a large bunch of keys, nearly dropping the huge loaf of bread tucked under her arm as she let herself in, before vanishing into the hall as she slammed the door shut.

"I wonder who *that* was; she looks pretty dire. I hope she's not Mrs Hart," Eve instantly thought, as the sight of the woman's mean face adhered to her mind.

A few seconds later, Eve glanced at her watch, and deciding the time had arrived to go into the house, she picked up her suitcase and entered the sizeable grounds, treading the red, gravelled path that led to the porch.

Once reaching the glass-fronted door, she rang on the bell. In seconds, the porch door unlatched; Eve finding herself face to face with a woman about her own age, dressed in a uniform similar to that of a nurse, consisting of navy blue trousers, a jumper, wax jacket and blue polo shirt. Recognizing the maid as a nanny, Eve realised a child inhabited the house, although nannies were sometimes employed to look after children older than seven since the engagement of household servants had been reintroduced.

"Are you the new lady's maid?" the nanny enquired, curiously eyeing Eve's case.

"I'm here to see Mrs Hart regarding the post," Eve politely replied.

"Oh, I see. If you'd like to come in and sit down,

I'll tell Mrs Hart you are here," the nanny replied as she pulled back the door.

The nanny led Eve into the lounge; nothing like the parlour or death rooms in Victorian times with embroidered, upholstered seats in velvet brocade, carved, marble-topped tables, traditional-styled lamps or porcelain jars with crocheted doilies beneath. The ceilings had no chandeliers; not one mirror possessed a frame in carved wood or gilt gold; nor were there grandfather clocks, stained glass windows or carpets with patterned designs.

The seating was placed in the core of the room - away from the naked white walls which had lighting all round. The sofa itself had also changed in design, and now consisted of moveable seats allowing for multiple needs, numerous layouts and various positions of use such as facing different directions, reclining or just sitting down. The marble, tiled flooring was also in white, partly offset by a rug in zigzag design lying under the seats; and it was here where Eve patiently sat, as the nanny submerged from the room to inform Mrs Hart that her interviewee had arrived.

Being a contemporary lounge, the room had no trinkets or shelves. Even the walls appeared typically bare - apart from one solitary frame containing the photograph of a young girl - which hung by the bar. As the frame caught her eye, Eve got up from her seat to take a closer look at the snapshot it housed. From afar, the girl had looked wholesome and pert, but presented a different impression to one standing near; for as charming and cute as the camera allowed her to seem, the look in her eyes appeared cunning and highly disturbed. The girl looked about twelve or thirteen, but the photograph could have been taken sometime ago.

"She's probably Mrs Hart's daughter," Eve thought, as she made her way back to the couch and positioned herself by her suitcase, facing the bar.

The click of the handle made her look up, as the nanny re-entered the lounge, wearing a look frustrated and worn, which she tried to conceal.

"Mrs Hart is ready to see you. If you'd like to come this way," the nanny announced with a sigh that she failed to suppress, as Eve rose from her seat, following her out of the room and into the hall.

As they ascended the stairs, the irate, sour-looking woman Eve saw entering the house whilst she waited outside, was on her way down, throwing the aspirant a glance of dislike as she passed. Eve longed to ask the young maid who this harsh woman was, but resolved to stay quiet as they reached the top of the stairs, to enter a passage with bubble-wrap wallpapered walls and a low, slanting roof.

There were quite a few rooms on this floor, and Eve noticed the disquieted look in the nanny's blue eyes as they passed the room with the notice pinned up on its door reading: *"Private; no entry permitted; do not disturb."*

"This is the mistress's study," the nanny announced, as they stopped at a room with a wood-panelled door that was painted in green. "She'll see you right now; just knock before entering the room," the nanny advised, retracing her steps down the hall once she wished Eve good luck.

Eve rapped a few times on the door, sidling into the room once Mrs Hart called out "Come in," to find herself facing a good-looking woman who had not quite reached middle age, dressed in the full-length leggings and long-length, tunic style top of contemporary years.

"Come and sit down," Mrs Hart said, pulling up a chair, before she and her interviewee took a seat at the desk.

"The agency sent on your CV," the mistress added, switching on her computer to search for Eve's record of work. "Ah - here it is," she went on, perusing Eve's file of employment through rigorous eyes.

161

"You are Eve Brent - and you've been a lady's maid to Mrs Hammond at Number 5, "Harlington Road" for the past four years and three months," the mistress resumed, leaving her laptop aside to focus on Eve, who felt she was staring her out.

"Yes," Eve succinctly replied, aware that the lady of the house was sizing her up.

Mrs Hart's penetrative stare shot through Eve's eyes, before making its way to her shoes and rumpled attire.

"The agency said Mrs Hammond gave you a character reference before you departed from her house; do you have it to hand?" the mistress enquired, refocusing her eyes on Eve's own.

"Yes," the other replied, taking out her ex-mistress's note from the side of her case.

"Thank you," Mrs Hart said, seizing the note from Eve's grasp before reading its words. "That's a very good reference indeed," the homeowner remarked, returning the note to her interviewee with a smile. "According to your former employer, you're polite, assiduous, discreet and efficient in your work - every asset in a lady's maid that a mistress would want. However, there is one point that we need to clear up," the mistress went on; her face forming into a frown as she stared at Eve's case. "I see by the case at your feet that you seem to have left your old job in a bit of a hurry: did you happen to do something Mrs Hammond didn't like?"

Eve's eyes flitted over the desk. She felt positively snared; unsure whether or not to provide Mrs Hart with the truth or to concoct a lie.

"Did you find my last question difficult to grasp?" Mrs Hart curtly asked, vexed that her interviewee had failed to reply.

"The last night I'd worked for the Hammonds, I had been out. The bus - which was usually on time - arrived five minutes late, and I got back to the house past the midnight curfew allowed. Other than that, I've obeyed and have pleased my ex-mistress throughout," Eve explained, deciding to opt for the truth.

Mrs Hart lowered her eyes, taking her time to think about what Eve had said before she replied.

"I have to admit, had *I* been your mistress, I wouldn't have been pleased," she coolly remarked. "I'm sure Mrs Hammond must have told you once you got back that even night buses run well before midnight, and that it would have been wiser and within your best interests to have caught an earlier bus. Moreover, being gone from her house that evening for quite a long time meant you weren't there to attend to her needs had she wanted your help: a very expensive mistake to have made on your part after more than four years."

"Mrs Hammond *did* give me a reference," Eve gently replied, feeling Mrs Hart had been far too hasty to judge. "Despite my single mistake, she wanted me to stay; but Mr Hammond insisted that I be replaced; so before I left, she wrote me a reference for future employment without his being aware."

"So had it not been for Mrs Hammond's husband, you'd still be employed at their house?" remarked Mrs Hart, eyeing the other in doubt.

"It's the truth," Eve earnestly stressed. "Mrs Hammond pleaded with her husband to keep me on and to let the matter go - but he just wouldn't bend."

Mrs Hart looked down at the desk, pausing once more to mull over what Eve had just said.

"You undoubtedly broke the rules by arriving back late," she finally replied, pinning her eyes back on Eve with a tentative sigh. "But I suppose that, taking your general loyalty and compliance towards Mrs Hammond into account, Mr Hammond could have agreed to let you stay on; but usually under *my* roof, a servant who doesn't abide by the rules doesn't last."

Eve threw Mrs Hart a faint smile, without being sure whose side the latter had been on - Mr Hammond's or his dutiful wife's.

"And I take it you've worked as a servant ever since you left school?" assumed Mrs Hart, changing the theme.

"Actually, no," Eve politely replied. "I originally trained as a white collar worker - and straight after college, spent a year keying in data for a firm selling cars."

"Oh?" uttered Mrs Hart in a tone of surprise.

"Then, of course the 2320 pandemic occurred," Eve abstractedly said, looking back on the past several years with regret. "I was furloughed by the firm, which - like a lot of businesses at that time - didn't stay afloat. By the time the pandemic died down and we came out of lockdown, unemployment was rife - and like many others, I couldn't get another job in the field in which I'd been trained; so I turned to the work I do now. Things haven't exactly been easy," she sadly went on, forgetting who she addressed.

Mrs Hart looked down again; and when she looked up, Eve saw that her eyes appeared moist and full of torment.

"I know what a curse that pandemic has been to us *all*. It claimed the life of my husband, and left me to bring up a daughter all on my own," the mistress replied with a frustrated sigh.

"I'm sorry; I had no idea," Eve guiltily said, regretting not having chosen her words with a little more care.

"OK, then, Eve. I'll phone you with my verdict today by a quarter to five," Mrs Hart coolly said, rising from her seat as Eve followed suit, seizing her suitcase in haste before reaching the door. "I trust you know your way out," the mistress went on, as Eve placed her hand on the knob, unkeen on the thought of working as Mrs Hart's maid if given the job, yet even more desperate to gain a roof over her head.

"Yes, thank you, Mrs Hart. Have a nice day," the aspirant replied, exiting the room to retrace her steps down the passage that led to the stairs she walked down before leaving the house.

🕐 🕐 🕐 🕐 🕐

Eve sat alone in the café close to the agency she had approached. She would have preferred to stay in the park, but needed to keep on her phone, which the owner allowed her to charge by the seat where she sat, waiting to hear Mrs Hart's decision regarding the post.

After perusing the newspaper left on her desk by a customer as she arrived, Eve glanced at the clock on the wall at the side of the bar, to see that the deadline had passed for the mistress to call.

"Has she not phoned you yet?" the proprietor asked as he stopped at her table to wipe it and clear it of cups.

"No," Eve wearily sighed, almost giving up hope.

"We'll be closing up soon. We open again tomorrow at 6am if you're at a loose end," he announced, eyeing her case.

"I *will* be for sure - if the mistress who interviewed me for the job decides not to call; and even if she *does*, she may well have picked someone else," Eve tensely replied, her dread of spending the beckoning night on the pavement or a park bench becoming acute.

"When you first came in here with that case, I thought you were back from a trip," the owner remarked, spraying and wiping more tables as he talked on. "I wish I could help you with finding somewhere to stay - but the truth is, I *can't*. If you can't afford a B&B, perhaps you could try the local workhouse instead, if you've nowhere to live."

165

"The *workhouse*?" Eve cried in dismay. "I've heard terrible rumours about what those places are like."

"Well, they're nothing as bad as they were in Victorian times," the proprietor stressed, "— and they *are* for those with no money to pay for their keep. Besides, they don't want to make things too cushy - or inmates won't want to get off their backsides and leave them to pay their own way."

Eve removed her charger from the wall, wondering where she could revive her phone once its battery ran down, as the last customer emptied his cup and abandoned his seat. As she picked up the phone to put it away, it suddenly started to ring; and as the hand of the clock slid to six, the proprietor held up his hand, granting her several more minutes to answer the call.

Eve pressed the button and held the phone to her ear in dread and suspense.

"Hello," she nervously said, as the owner submerged through the arch that stood next to the bar.

"Am I speaking to Eve?" the caller enquired.

"Speaking," said Eve, at once realising who called.

"It's Mrs Hart, regarding the lady's maid post," the other announced.

"Hello, Mrs Hart," Eve politely replied.

"I've interviewed three other people since having seen you," the homeowner said, only to pause, leaving Eve to wonder what would ensue. "It was hard to decide who to choose for the post in such limited time, but the vacancy had to be filled."

"I see," Eve downcastly replied, assuming by Mrs Hart's tone that she had not been picked.

"I was hoping to have met more suitable applicants for the post," Mrs Hart carried on, "but as I needed a maid straight away, I opted for *you*, since I felt you were the most suitable out of the four," she finally announced, as the owner reappeared with a set of keys in his grasp, waiting for Eve to depart so that he could lock up.

"Thanks very much for employing me, Mrs Hart," Eve respectfully said, without daring to ask the homeowner when she could start.

"Let's hope that I've made the right choice," Mrs Hart coolly said in response to Eve's gratified words. "Please bear in mind that as soon as you start, you'll be placed on a trial of three months - and if neither the housekeeper nor I are pleased with your work, you won't be kept on, I'm afraid," she flatly went on, warning Eve against feeling complacent too soon.

Seconds of silence ensued, during which Eve looked up; the proprietor reminding her it was time to lock up with one glance at his watch.

"I expect you're wondering when you can start," resumed Mrs Hart, as Eve held up her hand to the man with the keys as a sign that it would not be long before she would leave.

"Yes, Mrs Hart," replied Eve, careful of saying too much.

"As I need someone now, you can start straight away," the lady of the house firmly said, as the proprietor hovered close to Eve's seat with inquisitive eyes. "It's getting quite late; I want you round here so I can introduce you to the other members of staff who'll show you around the house before you start work: are you able to come straight away?"

"Yes, Mrs Hart; I'll be round in a few minutes' time," Eve intently replied, unsure by the mistress's tone that the job would work out, yet relieved to be certain of having a bed for the night.

"As soon as you are let in, come straight to my room in the attic where your interview was held. Once we've had a few words, you'll be shown to your room, where you can unpack and change into the outfit you are to wear in my house at all times," the mistress enjoined, as the proprietor pointed to his watch, prompting Eve to depart.

"Thanks, Mrs Hart; I'll be round very soon," Eve replied, ending the call and placing the phone in her bag before seizing her luggage and hurrying her way to the door.

"So you got the job, then?" the proprietor said, moving in on the door with his keys.

"Yes," Eve replied, as he turned the key in the lock.

"That must have come as a relief," he remarked, as Eve stepped out of the café and onto the street. "Mind you, I expect it's like treading on eggshells in those kind of jobs. I'm thankful for owning this café and having kept it afloat, when - thanks to the pandemic - so many businesses have had to shut down," he tactlessly added, lowering his eyes.

"Lucky you," Eve dryly remarked, turning quickly away to head for Mrs Hart's home in "Harpenden Road."

🕐 🕐 🕐 🕐 🕐

Eve unpacked her clothes which she placed in the closet of the sky-lighted room in the attic of Mrs Hart's house. She stored the rest of her things into the drawers before changing into the clothes that the lady's maid wore: black, long-length leggings, a tunic style top and an apron to match. Once placing her suitcase away, she heard a knock on the door; and a split second later, her mistress stepped into the room.

"Ah, Eve," Mrs Hart said, eyeing the bed to see it vacant of clothes. "Now you've unpacked and been shown where everything is, I can introduce you to the other members of staff."

"OK," murmured Eve, in dread of having to meet her co-workers without knowing why.

"Come this way," the homeowner said, as Eve followed her out of the room. "They're all waiting for you in the servants' hall, so we'd better go down," she went on as they walked down the passage in haste; her maid furtively eyeing the room labelled *"Private. No Entry. Do not disturb,"* as they passed.

The two women descended the stairs, Mrs Hart leading Eve to the door of a secluded room at the back of the house, knocking three times before she and her servant walked in.

"As you can see, only six employees live in; the casual members of staff I employ live elsewhere," Mrs Hart said to Eve, as they entered a room with a ceiling of pendant spotlight rotatable lamps and walls of 3D faux leather in lattice design.

Eve eyed the servants she faced, who stood side by side, in front of the long dining table surrounded by tulip style chairs. In the centre hovered a woman dressed in the long-length leggings and tunic style top that her counterparts wore, except for her uniform lacking the white linen apron the others had on; it was the sour-faced woman Eve saw bustling into the house.

"This is Eve," went on Mrs Hart, addressing her staff. "Now, Eve; let me introduce you to the principal servant of the house - my housekeeper, Miss Molloy," the homeowner said, Eve warily eyeing the woman whilst swallowing hard.

"Hello," said Eve, holding out her hand for the woman to shake.

Miss Molloy kept her hand by her side, throwing Eve another black look when meeting her eye.

"Hello," she hostilely said, eyeing the new maid from forehead to toe; Eve warily backing away, overwhelmed with unease.

"Miss Molloy is in charge of everyone here, except for

yourself; you are responsible to *me*. She also manages my bills, welcomes my guests and reports back to me on the running of the house every day," Mrs Hart said to Eve, who was thankful for not being under the housekeeper's 'care.'

Eve lowered her eyes, before shifting them to the cook's help, who threw her a smile.

"This is Ann. She helps out our cook with preparing our meals," Mrs Hart said, as the help accepted Eve's hand.

"Welcome aboard," greeted Ann.

"Nice to meet you," the lady's maid said, returning her smile before focusing on the woman beside the cook's help.

"This is Mary, our cook," the homeowner said, the former shaking Eve's hand after saying hello. "Mary's in charge when Miss Molloy's very busy or doesn't happen to be here," went on Mrs Hart, as Eve said hello before moving on to the next servant in line.

"This is my gardener, Jo. She resides in a lodge in the grounds at the back of the house," the mistress announced, referring to the butch-looking woman shaking Eve's hand.

"Hello, Eve; welcome to the team," the gardener pronounced.

"I'm pleased to be here," Eve replied, throwing Miss Molloy a tentative glance.

"Hello," greeted the final member of staff, who was the nanny in the blue shirt Eve had come by before.

"Eve and I have already met," said the nanny to Mrs Hart. "I'm Deborah; nice to have you as one of our team," she added, addressing the new employee, who threw her a smile as both servants shook hands.

"If you haven't eaten for hours, you can now join the rest of the staff for supper here in this hall, after which I'll need your assistance with a few things," Mrs Hart said to Eve as she walked to the door. "Take a seat at the table with Jo and Miss Molloy while Mary and Ann get supper prepared."

🕐 🕐 🕐 🕐 🕐

It was a quarter past eight. Eve had been freed from her tasks to retire for the night, and ascended the stairs to the attic, frayed from the stress she had borne for the past several hours.

As she walked down the passage, the click of an opening door encountered her ears, and she promptly turned round to see the door of the out-of-bounds room strangely ajar. Retracing her steps, she halted when nearing the door, feeling it wiser to shut it than leave it unclosed, for fear of being accused of entering the room.

As Eve reached for the handle, the door began to move back, edging increasingly open as each second passed; until out of the mystery room, a young girl nudging her teens, with ringlets and gold, lace-up shoes, slowly emerged.

"That's Mrs Hart's daughter," Eve thought, recognizing the face as the girl's in the frame she had seen in the lounge, as the youth mutely stood by the wall with malevolent eyes.

Eve felt herself backing away for fear of being seen near the girl by anyone climbing the stairs; and turning away, she walked on until reaching her room.

She twisted the handle and dared not look back, as she heard someone mounting the stairs; but froze on the spot as she felt that same person draw near.

"Hold it right there!" snapped a voice from behind, as she tensely turned round to face the formidable figure of Miss Molly with the ill-natured, straying young girl secured in her grasp.

"Like everyone else, you were strictly told not to enter this room," the housekeeper went on, pointing to the room from which the girl had emerged. "This isn't a very good start - having broken the rules on your very first night. Maybe you'd care to explain why you dared to waltz in."

"I *didn't* go into the room. As I came up the stairs, I saw that the door was shut; but then I heard it click open, and saw the young girl coming out as I passed," Eve innocently said, keeping her manner polite.

"How coincidental; in all the years I've been here, this has not happened before," the housekeeper barked, eyeing the young maid in doubt. "It's my duty to ensure that all goes well in this house, and to hunt out a member of staff who's not easy to trust. I'm sure you nosed into that room and let the girl out - which is a serious breach of the rules. I hope I don't have to report this to Mrs Hart," warned Miss Molloy, as the girl became fractious and let out a loud, piercing wail.

"I don't work under you," Eve began to protest. "I work under Mrs Hart. It's up to *her* to treat me as she sees fit."

"That still doesn't mean she hasn't the right to know what you did," the housekeeper snapped; the girl in her grasp growing increasingly wild.

"But I *didn't* enter the room; and it wasn't as if you were there at the time the door opened to prove it was me," Eve said in retort.

Miss Molloy narrowed her eyes, preparing to shout, only to be stopped by the girl biting viciously into her hand. Eve slowly drew back, and stretching her hand out behind her, twisted the handle and entered her room, hurriedly shutting the door as the housekeeper yelled out in pain before dragging the unruly girl back into her room.

Eve pressed the skylight control with a wavering hand, as the girl's interminable wail penetrated the walls of her room from the narrow passage beyond. She sat on the bed, fearful of being dismissed after what had just passed, as the screen of the skylight slid down and made the room dark. The screaming suddenly stopped as she heard a door close, followed by the patter of footsteps out in the hall that died down as they met with the stairs, to render the floor of the attic inactive again. Eve dared not depart from her room as the sound of her fellow members of staff entering their own encountered her ears. She was loath to come down to the hall and have breakfast with the head servant who wanted her out, and spent the night in suspense, without any sleep.

In the morning, she ventured downstairs, forcing herself to enter the long servants' hall. Miss Molloy stared her out without saying a word as she took her seat and they waited for all the others to enter the room. Once breakfast was over, Eve rose to exit the room, during which Miss Molloy spoke at last, causing the maid to halt and turn back as she came to the door.

"I've something to tell you before you waltz off," the housekeeper hostilely said.

"What's that?" Eve fearfully asked as she turned back.

"Mrs Hart wants to see you before you start work; you're to go to her now," the head servant announced; her juniors swapping staid looks but too frightened to speak.

Eve turned on her heels and rushed out of the hall, realising what Mrs Hart wished to see her about. Swallowing hard, she made her way to the lounge, where her mistress soberly sat, slowly raising her head as the servant appeared.

"Ah, Eve; thanks for arriving to see me so promptly," Mrs Hart said, as her lady's maid stood by the hearth suppressing her fears. "Come and sit down; I trust you

173

know what this is about," the mistress went on, pointing to the armchair facing her own.

Eve nodded without a reply, while taking her seat.

"I'm afraid there's a bit of a problem regarding an incident last night," Mrs Hart coolly pronounced. "It concerns the room in the attic one mustn't disturb. No one but Miss Molloy is allowed to go in; even Deborah, my nanny, hasn't been given the right. "But according to Miss Molloy, you'd been in it last night."

"As I passed the room on the way to my own, I saw that the door was ajar - and I felt it was better to shut it myself; but I never went in," explained Eve, finding it strange that the nanny had also been banned from the room.

"Miss Molloy said that on her way upstairs to the attic she saw you with your hand on the handle of the door, and that you were the only other member of staff on that floor at the time," Mrs Hart carried on, failing to mention the girl who had let herself out.

"I had my hand on the handle to *shut it* - not to go in. Did Miss Molloy not make it clear that she never actually *saw* me enter the room? Because she only saw me with my hand on the handle of the door," Eve politely affirmed, continuing to wonder why Mrs Hart had not referred to the girl.

"Yes, she did," the homeowner replied, pausing to study the servant she chose to employ. "And it's on this basis - and on the fact that you're responsible to *me*, and not Miss Molloy - that I've decided to let the matter go, and give you one further chance; but I warn you in future to leave the handle alone and to simply walk past - whether you happen to see the door open or not. If you touch it again, I'll have no choice but to ask you to leave."

"Thank you, Mrs Hart," Eve respectfully said; the fear that Miss Molloy may report her again for another 'mistake' staving off her relief.

"And now that we've cleared the matter up, I've a favour to ask," the mistress announced. "Something's come up, and Deborah has had to rush off to her parents in Hove - so won't be here for the day. *I* will also be out, so will need you to tend to my daughter, Candice, until I get back."

Eve instantly froze, fearful of having to handle the unruly girl who she saw in the attic the previous night.

"I have Candice here with me now, and would like you to meet her before I scoot off - that's if she'll choose to come in and stop hiding out in the hall," the mistress remarked, as Eve's dread continued to rise.

"Candice - come into the lounge at once!" Mrs Hart called; and seconds later, her daughter stepped into the room with a courteous smile; Eve repressing her shock as the girl caught her eye.

"Candice - this is my new lady's maid, Eve. Today you'll be under her care while Deborah is out," said Mrs Hart to her daughter - who was not the girl in the frame slipping out of the room the previous night, but another, aged about eight, with long, flaxen hair.

"Hello, Candice," greeted Eve, leaving her seat to approach the timid, young girl.

"Candice - say hello to Eve; I'm sure she won't bite," the girl's mother said, whereupon Candice dutifully whispered hello to the maid.

"I'll be gone in a few minutes," the homeowner said as she rose from her seat. "I won't be back before eight this evening - so keep Candice well entertained. She won't want to have lunch or tea in the dining hall alone - so get Mary and Ann to bring both your meals to the table - here in this lounge. Once you and Candice have finished your food, bring the empty plates back into the kitchen for Mary or Ann to wash up. Candice is terribly shy, but I'm sure that she'll like you in time. I've left a few board games on the table by the plant to occupy her mind; and if she gets bored, you can turn the television on; she may like to watch something on there. I've kept her off school today; she has a bit of a headache - but tomorrow I'm sending her back," the mistress went on, as her daughter furtively sidled back into the hall.

Mrs Hart made her way to the door, Eve hoping that Candice had not wandered too far.

"I'll pick up my coat from the hall, and then I'll depart. See you later on," Mrs Hart said, briefly turning back before leaving the front room in haste to exit the house.

As the front door clicked shut, Eve hurried into the hall, loath to be blamed if Mrs Hart's daughter had strayed from the house to be lost; but only a few minutes later, Candice emerged from the landing above, making her way down the stairs and back into the hall.

"Candice - come and sit in the lounge," the lady's maid called, steering the little girl into the room, as she saw Miss Molloy poke out her head from the top of the stairs in search of an error to report.

Eve was glad to be spending the hours that passed ensconced in the lounge with Candice - away from the housekeeper's spiteful, critical eyes; and it was a pleasure to look after such a tractable child that was blessed with a disposition so gentle and sweet. Eve was also relieved to savour her lunch with Candice in the lounge, rather than having to sit in the servants' hall with Miss Molloy and the other gossipy staff, who the chief maid had clearly told about what had occurred in the attic the previous night.

Once she and Candice had finished their lunch, Eve piled their plates on a tray, bringing them through to the kitchen for Ann to wash up. Miss Molloy stood by the stove, talking to Mary and one of the casual staff; the cook and housekeeper both falling quiet as Eve entered the room.

"Excuse me, Mary; there's something I've forgotten to do," the head servant piped up, throwing Eve a malevolent glance before leaving the room.

The lady's maid wondered where the housekeeper had gone, aware by the look on the faces of Mary and Ann that they knew Miss Molloy did not want her as part of the team. Minutes later, Eve had returned to the lounge to see Candice back on the couch, from which the young girl immediately rose as she saw her appear.

"Miss Molloy was in here while you took back our plates," the child naively remarked. "She told me to leave the room while she made a call on her phone. She got cross when I came back too early, and saw her standing in front of the cabinet drawer. I don't like Miss Molloy; I find her too strict; and because of her, Lex had to leave."

"Who was Lex?" Eve enquired as they both took a seat.

"She was the lady's maid Mum had employed before you. Miss Molloy got Mum to tell her to leave."

"Why was that?" Eve asked in dismay, wondering why Miss Molloy had entered the lounge while she took back the plates.

"Miss Molloy didn't like her, and told Mum she'd entered the room in the attic - the one where no one's allowed to go in. I pleaded with Mum not to tell her to go, as I thought Miss Molloy was being unfair; but Mum wouldn't listen and asked Lex to leave. Miss Molloy doesn't like *me* much, either - and I don't like *her*."

"Well, she doesn't seem to like *me*," Eve said with a sigh. "She wouldn't shake hands when I started work here, and has shown me hostility ever since - so much so that I hope I won't be the next servant to leave."

"*I* hope so, too; I want you to stay," the little girl earnestly said. "Some people are cold, and you're *not*."

"You're most kind to say so," said Eve. "But just

because you're nice doesn't mean to say you're not going to be sacked. I can only hope that Miss Molloy gets used to me in time."

The child grimaced in doubt, after which Eve looked down, thinking back to the girl she saw in the attic the previous night.

"Candice," the servant began, once several seconds had passed. "Who is that girl with the ringlets and the gold shoes? I saw her in the passage of the attic yesterday night."

Candice averted her eyes from the lady's maid's own.

"Mum has told me not to mention her, or to tell anyone who she is," said Candice, after a pause. "But if I told you a secret, would you promise not to tell?"

"I promise not to breathe a word," the maid earnestly said. "Is she your sister?"

"No. I'm Mum's only child. That girl who you saw in the attic isn't Mum's daughter; she's Miss Molloy's. That's why Miss Molloy is the only one who's allowed in that room; that's where the girl lives," the other declared.

Eve's eyebrows shot up in surprise at what Candice had said.

"But why is she being kept *here*?" she immediately asked, finding it strange that an offspring of Miss Molloy's was housed in one room - away from everyone else - under Mrs Hart's roof.

"Miss Molloy is a distant cousin of ours - so Mum felt obliged to help out; but I hate her so much, that I don't consider her any relation *at all*," Candice glumly replied. "That daughter is mad, uncontrollably rough, and a danger to everyone else. But her mother won't have her locked up - so keeps her upstairs. That's probably why Miss Molloy's so moody and cross all the time, and takes it out on everyone else."

"Oh, I see," murmured Eve, unnerved that the room where she slept was a few doors away.

Eve and Candice spent the next few hours playing draughts; and just before supper, the mistress returned, entering the lounge as soon as she arrived to greet her daughter and hand her a packet of sweets.

"No opening these before supper," she said to the child, throwing her servant a smile before saying hello.

"Mum - can Eve look after me again?" Candice pleadingly asked; shifting her large, wistful eyes back on the maid.

"No, Candice," her mother gently replied. "Eve works strictly to me, I'm afraid. *Deborah's* your nanny; she'll be back tomorrow to tend to you straight after school. Has she been good?" the mistress asked Eve, with another brief smile.

"Impeccably; this has been more like a day of leisure than anything else," the servant replied.

"Well, unfortunately, Eve, you're here to look after *me*," the mistress affirmed, reminding her maid that she had no choice in the duties she had to perform.

Moments of silence ensued, after which Mrs Hart spoke again, as the sound of footsteps descending the stairs met her ears.

"It's almost time for my staff to be relieved of their duties for the night. Why would one of them wish to see me at such a late hour?" she bafflingly asked.

But on hearing that sound, Eve was not puzzled at all, freezing in dread as she realised which servant it was, and why that employee had dared to disturb Mrs Hart at such a late hour.

"Mrs Hart!" called a voice from the hall amidst successive raps on the door, which her mistress pulled open in haste. "Mrs Hart, this is urgent!" went on Miss Molloy as she barged her way into the lounge.

"What is it, Miss Molloy? Couldn't it have waited until the morning?" Mrs Hart curtly asked, feeling put out.

"Mrs Hart," Miss Molloy persevered, "Please look in your cabinet drawer where you've kept all your cash. Earlier on, when I pulled it open to check that the money was there, I found it had gone!"

"Gone?" her mistress exclaimed. "How on earth can that be?"

"The drawer's empty, Mrs Hart; its best that you check it for yourself," the housekeeper urged, prompting her mistress to make her way to the cabinet in haste.

"You're right; the money's disappeared!" the homeowner gasped, as she opened the drawer to find that its contents were gone. *"You* were in here with my daughter today; did you know about this?" she immediately asked, turning her focus on Eve, whom she promptly approached; while the housekeeper stood, gloating, a stone's throw away.

"No. I never went *near* that cabinet drawer; I wasn't even aware it contained any cash," Eve replied in despair, as she guessed what Miss Molloy must have spitefully done.

"It *must* have been her. *She* was the only servant in here all day; the other members of staff, including myself, have been working elsewhere," the housekeeper cut in.

"It *wasn't* her, Mum!" Candice said, in an effort to take up for Eve. "I've been with her all day - and Miss Molloy came down here just after lunch. Miss Molloy told me to leave the room before she came in; and when I returned to the lounge, I saw her standing in front of the cabinet drawer."

"And what were you doing coming into this lounge, standing by the cabinet drawer?" the mistress enquired, turning to Miss Molloy with distrustful eyes.

"I came into this room to make a personal call on my phone, Mrs Hart; I didn't want others listening in," the housekeeper replied.

"So you order my daughter out of a room in the house that her own mother owns so that they *don't*?" Mrs Hart crossly asked. "There are quite a few rooms in this house; there was no need whatsoever for you to have made your call *here*."

"I'm sorry, Mrs Hart. It won't happen again," the housekeeper unctuously said, as Eve threw her glance of uneasy mistrust.

"And where were *you*, Eve, when all this occurred?" Mrs Hart asked her personal maid, who wondered how the confrontation would end.

"Candice and I had just finished our lunch - and I'd gone to the kitchen to hand back the plates to be washed," Eve replied with unease, aware that her mistress was not in the happiest of moods.

"That's fair enough, I suppose, since *I* was the one who told you and Candice to have lunch in the lounge," remarked Mrs Hart; Eve feeling relieved that her mistress had seemed to calm down.

"But Mrs Hart - what about your money?" cut in Miss Molloy, peeved that the mistress had focussed her anger on her. "It's all gone missing; aren't you concerned?"

"I was coming to that," the homeowner said, shifting her eyes to the cabinet drawer as she spoke. "Miss Molloy - when did you find that my money was missing from the drawer?"

"Just after lunch - after making my personal call," the housekeeper replied, glancing at Eve with sly, malevolent eyes. "I made my way into the lounge, and found Candice sitting alone; and it seemed that Eve took her time getting back to the room - leaving the child unattended, and wondering where she had gone. I'd guess that Eve had slipped up to her room."

"What makes you say *that*, Miss Molloy?" the mistress perplexedly asked.

"Because, Mrs Hart, I think you should check in Eve's bedroom, as well as my own, to see if the pilfered cash is in any of the drawers. *I* wouldn't mind if you did, having nothing to hide," the housekeeper replied.

"Well, it's worth a look, I suppose," remarked Mrs Hart. "Because standing here asking questions to see who's the thief is getting me nowhere at all. Both of you - follow me up to the attic at once," she crossly went on, flouncing out of the lounge to be followed upstairs by Eve and the harsh Miss Molloy.

"We'll check your room first, Miss Molloy," advised Mrs Hart, as the three women came to the housekeeper's door while she took out the keys.

They entered the room; Eve and Miss Molloy standing back, as their mistress searched through the closet, drawers and neat grid of shelves fitted under the low, sloping roof.

"There's no money in *this* room; we'll go into Eve's," the mistress decidedly inferred, as the servants followed her out of the door and into the passage to head for the Eve's bedroom a few doors away.

"All this unnecessary bother - all because I can't trust my staff," the homeowner said, as she turned the key in the lock and marched into Eve's room.

Eve and the housekeeper followed her inside, Miss Molloy's sour face forming into a smirk as her mistress pulled open Eve's drawer to discover a bundle of twenty pound notes lying within.

"Just as I thought," the housekeeper remarked, ignoring Eve's presence as if she were not in the room.

"Is *this* why you'd vanished from the lounge for so long after lunch?" the mistress accusingly asked, turning to Eve, who was riddled with shock and dismay.

"I never went up to my room after lunch - and I'd kept my door locked," Eve innocently said, knowing that Miss Molloy kept a copy of her key. "I only went into the kitchen to hand back the plates, and was missing from the lounge for only a very short while."

"Well, according to Miss Molloy, you were missing for longer than that," opposed Mrs Hart; her large, baby blue eyes riddled with doubt. "Miss Molloy's been working for me for quite a few years - and I know how trustworthy she is. Can you give me one reason why I should take your word over hers - after happening to find my lost money stashed in your drawer?" she asked, as the housekeeper slyly looked on.

"Yes, actually, I *can*!" Eve cried in despair, knowing she would never be believed. "Your money could have been taken and put in my drawer by somebody else! Miss Molloy hasn't liked me from the moment I arrived, and has done nothing but try and trip me up. It's not as if she didn't have a copy of the key to my room," she went on, eyeing the culprit, who mutely stood at her side.

The mistress's eyebrows shot up; her expression suggesting that Eve had spoken out of turn.

"Thanks, Miss Molloy; that'll be all," she tersely announced; the housekeeper leaving the room without breathing a word. "Come back downstairs," the mistress went on, turning promptly to Eve after seizing the cash.

They descended the stairs and returned to the lounge, Candice turning her head as she saw them come in. Mrs Hart did not sit down, nor did she offer her servant a seat, as the two women stood, face to face, by the cabinet drawer.

"I think you're aware of what I'm going to say," the homeowner said, placing the bundle of cash back in the drawer from which she removed a square card. "I'm afraid that in the light of what's just been discussed, I must ask you to leave," she coolly went on, as the tears welled up in Eve's eyes. "I'm sorry things failed to work out - but servants who steal are never kept on; and you know I can't give you a reference after all this?"

"Yes, I'm aware," Eve hoarsely replied, lowering her eyes.

"I'll pay you up to the end of the week," the mistress declared, handing the servant her P45. "After breakfast tomorrow, I'll give you some time to pack all your things, and then you can go; is that understood?"

"It is," answered Eve, her eyes now on Candice, who sprang from the sofa in tears.

"Eve - I don't want you to go!" cried the child, running up to the maid whom she hugged, whilst sobbing out loud. "Mum - please don't make her go; I want her to stay!" begged Candice in vain, as her mother held up a stern, inflexible hand.

"Candice - you shouldn't be in here right now; please go upstairs to your room. I'll call you when you can come down," enjoined Mrs Hart, whereupon Candice immediately obeyed, running out of the front room in haste with red, swollen eyes.

🕐 🕐 🕐 🕐 🕐

Eve went without breakfast after a night of unrest; the thought of sitting in the servants' hall with Miss Molloy and the rest of the staff proving too much to bear. She had got up at dawn while the others were asleep, and packing her suitcase as soon as she could, had slipped out of the side of the house so as not to be heard.

With little cash in her purse and nowhere to go, she made her way into the park facing the café where she had received Mrs Hart's call. She spent the next hour glued to the bench, until seeing the café blinds lift, and the owner's industrious hand throw her a wave. His face formed into a frown as he noticed the case of belongings at her feet, after which she saw him beckoning her forth to come in.

Eve picked up her case, dejectedly crossing the road as he unlocked the door.

"Come on, get in," he said with a sigh as she trudged her way in, plumping down on the first chair she saw with fatigue. The proprietor stood by her seat, studying her red, swollen eyes with inquiring concern.

"You've been crying; been fired again?" he presumed, looking down at her case.

Eve mutely looked down, wiping a residual tear from her tired, troubled face.

"What happened *this* time?" he asked, eyeing the clock as he saw people gather outside.

"I was framed for stealing the money my mistress, Mrs Hart, had kept in her cabinet drawer," the other replied with a sigh of despair.

"By whom?" the proprietor asked in a tone of dismay.

"The housekeeper, Miss Molloy," Eve glumly replied. "She was full of active ill-will, and disliked me right from the start. Yesterday, while my mistress was out, and I was out of the lounge, she slipped into the room where I slept, placing the money into the drawer opposite my bed for Mrs Hart to conveniently find after searching the rooms."

"Dear, oh, dear; there are some nasty people out there who won't live and let live," said the owner, shaking his head as he took out the keys.

"So I've learned; and I haven't even been given a reference this time, so how will I find another job?" Eve sorely replied.

The proprietor lowered his eyes, emitting a tedious sigh before looking up.

"As soon as I saw you, I knew that the job you'd gone for wouldn't work out," he resignedly said; the usage of neighbourly tact escaping his mind. "Even though I don't know you, I've met many types - and could tell you were never cut out to be somebody's maid. I bet that wasn't the job you'd done from the start: do I happen to be right?"

"I started out in an office, keying in data for a firm selling cars; but since having been made redundant because of the pandemic, office jobs have been scarce."

"I'd figured as much," the owner remarked, placing a cruet stand on each table with diligent hands. "You don't seem the mealy-mouthed type, as polite as you are; and someone like Mrs Hart would find it even harder to stoop and obey - having been used to lounging around and giving the orders all day. Couldn't you give seeking office work one more go?"

"I've tried," Eve frustratingly sighed. "But since the pandemic, white collar jobs have been few and far between, as so many firms have closed down: there are hundreds of applicants fighting for one office post."

"Well, maybe you need to try harder; and now you've no reference for another domestic job, I'd say you had nothing to lose," the proprietor stressed, placing the last cruet set on the table near the door.

"What - without somewhere to stay?" Eve tensely exclaimed. No office would even consider employing a person without an address."

"I tell you what," the owner piped up. "The flat above this café is vacant; I have my own house a few streets away. You can stay here for a while if you like. I won't keep anyone permanently, mind - but you're welcome to stay here for now."

"Are you sure?" Eve asked in surprise, desperate for somewhere to live, at least for a few nights.

"I never say what I don't mean; *of course* you can stay," the owner earnestly stressed. "But while you're living at this address, drop round to the workhouse down the road, and try for accommodation *there*."

"Yes," Eve dully replied, not keen on the thought.

"Have you had any breakfast?" the proprietor asked, seeing it was time to open up.

"No; nor do I want anything to eat right away," Eve flatly replied, as he eyed the huddle of customers waiting outside.

"I tell you what," he proposed, edging closer to the door. "You can have lunch here, when you're ready - on the house; and once the café's less busy, you can make your way up to the flat and unpack your case. In the meantime, you can sit here, and I'll bring you over a coffee or tea once I've let in the queue. What's your name, by the way?"

"Eve - and thanks for being so kind," the other replied, wondering how long the owner would allow her to stay whilst he reached the door which he unlocked in haste, letting his customers in to queue at the bar.

In the next fifteen minutes, the waitress appeared; the chef having let himself in through the door at the rear; and during a lull at 10.30am, the proprietor led Eve upstairs to show her the flat, introducing himself as George before going downstairs to let her unpack. The flat itself was quite big, containing two bedrooms, a kitchen, a bathroom and sizeable lounge that looked onto the street.

Eve went into the bathroom where she placed two towels and a small bar of soap, provided by George before he went back downstairs; and choosing the smaller bedroom out of the two, she unzipped her suitcase and hung up her clothes, dogged by insecure thoughts and feelings of fear. For as kind as the owner had been, he was not going to house her for long; and the prospect of life in a workhouse filled her with dread.

Eve stayed in the flat until quarter to twelve before coming downstairs to the café for a late breakfast of mushrooms, bacon, fried bread and fresh scrambled eggs.

By one fifteen, she was facing the vast workhouse grounds, taking her time to advance after losing her nerve. At one thirty, she walked through the gates, sensing her leggings and tunic style top looked too smart as she entered the foyer and filled in a form of admission declaring her name, age, religion, marital status, previous address, and whether or not she had lived in a workhouse before. Two additional questions remained at the foot of the form pertaining to why she applied for admission, and her next of kin.

As she sat outside the Reviewing Officer's room waiting to be seen, the window beside her provided a view of the grounds; a chapel and ward for the sick occupying each end. Inmates were entering and leaving the building during her wait, all dressed in overalls made of grey canvas and calico cloth. Those straying in had a pass; some of them physically or mentally flawed in some way: those whom employers would not see fit to keep on, or even recruit. Most of these inmates were women; some of them old and infirm, whose pensions were not substantial enough to cover the cost of lodgings or homes of their own.

Within the next hour, Eve sat at the Officer's desk, as he and the Principal studied the form she filled out, whilst asking her numerous questions about her current state of affairs, and why she wanted to make the workhouse her home. She explained how she had lost her two previous jobs, and how leaving the latter without a reference had left her without much chance of being re-employed; how her only relations could not keep her under their roof as they lived far away, and that George had allowed her to stay in his vacant flat only until she had found somewhere else to reside.

She arrived back at the flat at a quarter to three; George too busy serving those lining his pockets to ask how her interview went. She stayed upstairs in the flat until 7pm, after which she came down - when the café had emptied and George was about to lock up.

"So how did things go?" he finally asked, bolting the door before fetching his coat.

"It's hard to tell," Eve vaguely replied. "I filled in a form, and the Reviewing Officer and head of the workhouse asked me a number of questions as they took notes. They said that in roughly two weeks, I'll be called back, and will go before a board ---."

"A Board of Guardians?" George rightly assumed.

"Yes; they are the ones to decide whether or not the workhouse is going to take me in," Eve dully replied, as the proprietor buttoned his coat and pocketed the keys.

"I'll keep my fingers crossed for you - and if you're successful, then at least you'll have somewhere to stay." the owner replied.

"Yes - but what if the Board turn me down?" Eve fearfully asked, hoping that George would soften and say she could stay in the flat for as long as she wished.

"I'd cross that bridge when you come to it," he bluntly replied, unwilling to discuss whether or not he would let her stay on if the Board of Guardians decided to turn her away.

"Have you had any supper?" George asked, changing the subject as soon as he could.

"No, I haven't," Eve faintly replied, struggling to quell her dismay at his callous response.

"I've a few packaged sandwiches here. Their use-by date is today; and they'll only be binned if you don't have them now - ham, chicken salad, plus coleslaw and cheese," the proprietor said, picking the food items up from under the bar.

"Thanks," Eve replied, as George placed the left-over food in a brown paper bag which he gave her in haste.

"Got to go; see you tomorrow," he said, submerging through the arch by the bar to make his way out from the back.

Eve pulled open the door that led to the stairs, and made her way up to the flat, thankful, at least, for the residual snacks she was given for free. Once devouring the sandwich with ham, she gulped down a chipped mug of tea and retired to bed, suffering an uneasy night of ominous dreams.

🕐 🕐 🕐 🕐 🕐

Eve had received her letter from 'Workhouse Admissions' before time - a week after her first interview took place. Three days later, she appeared before the Board to be brutally grilled on her state of affairs, and her reasons for being so desperate to find a free home. The meeting lasted for over an hour, held in a small, stuffy room at the workhouse's rear; a far more daunting ordeal than she thought it would be during which she was warned about how distressing entering a workhouse could be for those moving in.

Seven days later, the Board called her back to announce their decision to let her live under their roof, after which she was shown round its grounds by a member of staff who languidly pointed out the facilities it owned: the large dormitory where female inmates would sleep; the vast dining hall by the kitchen where they ate their meals; the recreation hall where they gathered after work; the allotments where vegetables were grown to be packaged and sold, or prepared by the kitchen for hungry inmates and staff. But nowadays, schools did not exist in the grounds; child inmates attending neighbourhood schools beyond the workhouse domain.

Following her tour of the workhouse, Eve returned

home, having been told by the Board that she was to move in once receiving their letter confirming what they had told her when calling her back; and she returned to her temporary flat dreading the day when that verifying note would arrive.

A few evenings later, she came downstairs to see that a litter of mail had been pushed through the door after George had gone home; and whilst seizing each item of post, she saw that the note from the Board of Guardians had already come. She opened the envelope up, as within her, a grudge against George began to take shape. Since having observed how decrepit the workhouse appeared, she sensed that this man was not as humane as he seemed. He had known what workhouses were like, but had led her to think their conditions were better than they were - a cruel ruse to dispense with her presence as soon as he could.

Placing the rest of the post to one side, she went back upstairs; reading the letter in the flat that she had to vacate. Once having perused the last line, she entered the bedroom and unzipped her case, packing away her belongings with cross, bitter thoughts.

The following morning, when George arrived at the café, she came back downstairs; her resentment reaching its peak as she showed him the note.

"Oh, so you've received the letter already? Are you all packed and ready to leave?" he typically asked, as Eve stood by the bar feeling her indignance rise.

"Packed but not ready," she dryly replied, seizing the note from his grasp.

"What do you mean 'you're not ready?'" he quizzically asked. "The workhouse requires you *now*."

"I'll *never* be ready," she said in retort. "I saw how dire the workhouse appeared when I was shown round; and besides, the Board of Guardians have warned me how shameful and stressful moving into a workhouse can be."

George paused from his usual tasks, turning to face the young woman with wide, aggrieved eyes.

"You ought to be grateful that I took you in. If it hadn't been for me, the workhouse would have had to take you in from the streets," he reproachfully said, turning back to his tasks with a disgruntled sigh.

"*Grateful*?" Eve quizzically cried, taking a nauseous glance at the note. "I've hardly been staying in your flat for five minutes - but it seemed even *that* was too long. You've wanted shot of me as soon as you could. The flat will stay empty *again* when I'm gone - so why didn't you let me stay on until I found a more decent abode?"

"Now hang on a minute; you've missed something here," the proprietor said, turning to face Eve once more, "You're *nothing* to me - not a mother, sister or niece; no relation *at all*. You're not even someone I've known - so what else did you expect - for me to have kept you on in the flat forever free of charge - from the kindness of my heart? You can't go round thinking life owes you favours; had *I* thought like that, I wouldn't be running this café *today*. If you don't like the thought of the workhouse, then hunt down a job to pay for a better abode."

"But who's going to employ me without a reference? And since the 2320 pandemic, unemployment's been rife. I couldn't exactly have found another job in a week to have moved out of *here*." Eve heard herself cry.

"Which doesn't mean to say that a comfortable abode's going to drop in your lap," George firmly snapped back. "I've outgoings to pay. Don't you realise how much the cost of my bills here has soared since you've been staying in the flat? Hasn't that ever crossed your mind? No - I didn't think it *had*. Now if you wouldn't mind, I've a café to run - so go up and check that you've packed all your things, and then leave."

Eve felt entirely crushed, as George turned his back before marching into the room at the rear to check in with the chef; whilst Eve went back upstairs to pick up her case, before leaving the café for good without saying goodbye.

The probation ward, where Eve had been housed soon after she arrived, was based near the front of the grounds - next to the room where her admissions hearing was held. She and six other new inmates were ordered to shower on their first day, after which each was given the standard uniform to wear. Eve had felt as if she were in prison as soon as her clothes were seized by the staff - to be washed, disinfected and put into store with the other belongings she owned, after having been told they would be returned on the day she would leave.

Eve would often converse with Sally - an inmate who slept in the neighbouring bed - who had lost many jobs through being anxious and shy. Sally eventually fell into debt, losing her home and the valuable respect of her family and friends, who had failed to take her condition into account. A breakdown and nowhere to stay had left Sally with no other choice but to turn to the workhouse for help; and sometimes when both inmates spoke, Sally would air how bitter she felt about the unfairness of life on the anxious and mentally ill.

"You know, if you are handicapped, anxious or mentally ill in some way, you're more likely to end up in here," she told Eve one morning during the break. "It's those who are able-bodied and mentally sound that live the best lives. Even before the pandemic, when one could draw dole, it used to be hard -- with those people

193

holding down jobs; getting four times as much every week; but since benefits were axed, things have become even worse. It's most humiliating coming in here after losing everything you had."

"I can imagine how the afflicted and mentally ill must be the first to suffer whenever things become tough. They must lack the resilience that others possess to survive," Eve humanely replied.

"You've got it in one," Sally said with a sigh. "But there's no way the Government will help. The pandemic put paid to that - draining the economy the way that it did so that benefits had to be axed; and it'll be yet *another* hard grind tomorrow - peeling potatoes all day."

"And the day after that, we'll be joining the men to chop wood; but at least that reduces the stress," Eve replied, as she and Sally drained their chipped mugs of insipid, stewed tea.

"I suppose," Sally tensely replied, as they saw a member of staff pop his head through the door.

"Hey, ladies; haven't you heard? The 'Space-age Trolls' are in town, and are now in the hall. Do you want to see them perform before turning in?" he excitedly asked; the two women eyeing him blankly with vacuous eyes.

"'The 'Space-age Trolls?' - who are they?" Sally cluelessly asked.

"Haven't you heard of the 'Space-age Trolls'? They're a group of travelling performers; all-rounders, they are. They sing, act, recite poems and plays, and tell all sorts of jokes; they're absolutely ace. You'd be mad to give them a miss," the staff member replied.

Feeling obliged to accept his proposal, the newcomers rose from their chairs and followed him into the hall, into which droves of inmates emerged, as Eve and Sally sat down on two seats that formed part of the row positioned nearest the stage. As the lights were dimmed and the curtain was raised, the performers were finally revealed; each member wearing a space-age suit and high, matching boots in metallic silvery grey. As the spotlights came on and lit up the stage, each face became visibly clear, causing Sarah to start and fall back in her chair as the group burst into song.

"Sally - what's wrong?" whispered Eve, seeing the look of utter dismay in the inmate's brown eyes.

"Him! That man on the left at the very far end; he's my ex-boss!" Sally bitterly breathed; her expression of shock transforming to one of dislike.

"What *about* him?" Eve curiously asked through the music that blared.

Without a reply, Sally abruptly stood up, turning innumerable heads as her ill feeling peaked.

"*You're* the reason I've ended up here!" she furiously cried; her voice surpassing the din of the music, which suddenly stopped, as she pointed a censuring finger at her ex-boss. "I lost everything I owned because you kicked me out without caring where I'd end up. I bet it made you feel big when you told me I wasn't confident enough to get away with making the errors the other staff made. You biasedly let them stay on - but got rid of *me* because of my nerves. Are you proud of ruining my life?" she went on, shedding indignant tears.

The rest of the inmates looked on - too downcast and lacking in pride to intrude or join in, as Sally was seized by both arms by two members of staff and brutishly dragged from the hall, leaving Eve sitting alone by a desolate seat.

Within moments, order returned and the music resumed; but feeling concerned for Sally, Eve rose from her seat and slipped out of the hall, heading for the dormitory in haste to see if she was there. She pushed open the door and walked down the large room of beds to find no one inside; and half an hour later, the head of the workhouse walked in to see her lingering alone by Sally's void bed, looking deeply perturbed.

"What brings you *here*, when everyone's still in the hall?" the Principal asked.

"Where's Sally?" Eve heedlessly said, turning to face him with wide, inquiring eyes.

"Why are you asking?" he said, as if the matter were not her concern.

"I was with her in the hall a few minutes ago, when she saw her ex-boss on the stage and grew terribly upset. It greatly alarmed me to see her removed from the hall," Eve replied, wondering where Sally had gone.

"Sally is an epileptic," the head of the workhouse declared. "She suffered a seizure after her outburst, and was brought to the hospital ward in the grounds to be nursed."

"Can I see her?" Eve worriedly asked, suspecting the shock of seeing the man who dismissed her had prompted the fit.

"No," the head curtly replied. "Sally's since had another seizure since having been brought to the ward. She's suffered a memory lapse, and is tired and confused; so she's being kept in for a while to recover and rest - and mustn't be disturbed."

Eve recalled how ill-starred her own job encounters had been over the past several weeks, sadly reflecting that Sally may not have survived had she been in her shoes. George would never have empathized, having been the type to 'hire and fire' without any qualms; and neither Mrs Hart nor the mistress who axed her for missing the night bus and getting back late would have ever agreed to take Sally on because of her nerves. Miss Molloy, too, would have grossly ill-treated her prior to forcing her out.

"It was the sight of her previous boss that drove her to this!" Eve crossly remarked, remembering what Sally had said about having lost jobs due to suffering from nerves. "Sally told me she'd been sacked from *other* workplaces as well; her employers weren't content until losing the poor girl her home and everything she owned - to end up in here. After suffering unfortunate experiences in my last two places of work, I know how she feels."

"You only get out of a job what you're willing to put in. As an employer myself, I refuse to keep members of staff who won't pull their weight," the head of the workhouse coldly replied.

"I'm referring to a point less tangible than that," Eve rejoined. "I'm referring to how unfairly employers treat staff who are anxious, mentally ill, or have low self-esteem. Didn't you hear Sally say in the hall that she couldn't get away with making mistakes that less anxious, more confident workers were permitted to make? What's *that* got to do with hard work? There must be plenty of inmates in here who've been through the same thing; they must still feel sorely aggrieved - and like Sally, it must make them ill."

The Principal threw Eve a negative glance, resenting the fact that a penniless inmate kept under his roof was candidly speaking her mind.

"I think you're addressing the wrong man," he scathingly said. "It's not up to this workhouse to see that employers keep our less confident inmates in work, and treat them with care and respect. We exist merely to feed them and keep a roof over their heads in exchange for the work they do *here* - for not being employed *elsewhere* - as benefits no longer exist. You, yourself, look perfectly wholesome to me - wholesome enough to find work and housing elsewhere if you feel that the way that this workhouse is run isn't meeting your needs."

The head briskly turned on his heels and stomped out of the room, as Eve retired for the night, lying awake by the vacant bed in which Sally had soundlessly slept the previous night.

During breakfast the following morning, Eve was called out of the hall to be led by a member of staff into the foyer, where a visitor sat, waiting for her to arrive. As Eve appeared, the visitor came into view; a young woman slightly older than herself with dark, shoulder-length hair and a bold, friendly face, dressed in leggings and a tunic style top partly cloaked by a light, summer coat.

"Jane! What are *you* doing here? Have you come back to this country to live?" Eve cried in surprise, facing the sister with whom she grew up, but now hardly saw.

"If I had have come back, I'd have told you," Jane said with a smile as she rose from her seat. "Is there somewhere quieter where we can talk?"

"The gardens, near the chapel," Eve softly replied, leading her sister out of the foyer to take the short cut.

In seconds they came to the plot and sat down on the bench facing the chapel where inmates would come twice a week, begging the Maker to take them away from the 'life' they endured."

"How did you know I was here?" Eve quizzically asked.

"I *didn't* at first," Jane replied with an uneasy grin. "I thought you still worked at the household in "Harlington Road." But when I came to the house, your ex-mistress said that you'd left, but that she didn't know where you'd gone, or where you were now. I was lucky; I happened to go into a café down the road for coffee and cake; and when I expressed my concern to the man who served me about not being able to find you, he told me you were here. I was taken aback; I didn't realise you'd ---"

Eve's sister paused, averting her eyes from the unadorned chapel ahead.

"— come to this," Eve baldly replied, completing Jane's unfinished words. "Since having left "Harlington Road," I've lost two jobs in a matter of only a few days," she tiredly went on, too crestfallen and listlessly drained to feel any shame. "The previous job lasted only a day, after I was wrongly accused of stealing some cash from my mistress's drawer - for which I was sacked without a reference to find future work. In days, I ran out of money - and ended up here."

"You've really been through it," Jane ruefully said. "How long have you been here?"

"Three weeks," Eve dully replied. "I'm in the probation ward; and you still haven't told me why you came all the way here," she curiously went on.

"I could have written and told you, I suppose. "But I'd planned to come here on a trip, so thought I'd tell you in person, instead," her sister replied.

"Tell me *what*?" Eve enquiringly asked.

"I've some family news about which you'll be saddened to hear," Jane sorely replied, pausing to stare into Eve's curious eyes. "Last week, Aunt Wyn passed away; she'd been ill for some time, as you know."

Eve lowered her head; her eyes stinging and moist.

"I didn't even get the chance to say goodbye. I feel that I have nothing left, and that I'm losing everyone dear," Eve sourly said, remembering how George had coldly expressed that he owed her no help, as she had been no one to him.

"I know this is sad," Jane gently replied, "But Aunt Wyn didn't fail to forget us just before she died; she has left us something to remember her by."

"What's *that*?" Eve passively asked, overcome by the run of ill luck she had recently borne.

"She's left us both something in her will - having had

no children of her own. I was surprised at how generous she'd been, when hearing what it was."

"What did she leave us?" Eve languidly asked, wryly believing Aunt Wyn's endowment would not be sufficient to dig her out of her plight.

"She's left us each half of her second abode - the house she and Uncle Clyde used as a retreat."

Eve abruptly looked up, finding it hard to take her sister's words in.

"What - that huge house in Leamington Spa? It's worth hundreds of thousands of pounds!" she gasped in surprise.

"*I* was shocked, too, when I heard," her sibling replied. "The funeral's being held at the end of this week; I'll send on some flowers from us both, and will cover the cost, as I know how you're placed. If the workhouse grants you leave, you can come with me to the funeral, of course; do you think you'll be able to attend?"

"I *must*; it's my duty to come," Eve staunchly replied. "Where's it being held?"

"In Newbury Heath - near where she lived," Jane confirmed, aware that her sister may find it a long way to come. "Don't worry; I'll still be here this Friday; we can both meet at Cambridge Heath Station and go there by train," she kindly assured.

"Oh, Jane!" Eve exclaimed, overcome with relief. "I can't believe this is happening; but it hurts to have lost one of the few in my life who genuinely cared," she sorely went on, bearing in mind how quickly George had turned cold.

"I know," Jane sadly agreed. "And I realise how much Aunt Wyn will be missed. But I know she'll have wanted us both to be happy; to grieve for her for a while; then live our lives, and move on."

"I suppose," Eve softly replied, reflecting that minutes

ago, she was dogged by the dread of having to live in want for the rest of her life.

"Now that I know where you're staying, I'll inform the solicitors of your change of address - and they'll send you a letter regarding the will very soon. Of course, it will be some time before everything comes through - and Aunt Wyn's house will have to be sold. Do you think you'll be able to find work between now and then?" Jane carefully asked.

"It doesn't look like I *will*. I can't go back to being a servant without a reference - and since the pandemic, most office jobs have dried up," Eve resignedly said.

"Do you think you'd be able to stick living here for the next several months?" her sister enquired, looking at her with concern.

"It looks like I'll *have* to," Eve tiredly replied, sour about having been axed from her previous job for an odious act that she did not commit. "But now, at least I can see a way out."

"Does your shift begin now?" Jane asked, seeing Eve eye the church clock.

"Yes," the other replied, as the two siblings rose from the bench. "I've to spend the whole day in the yard, chopping up wood."

In seconds, they bid each other goodbye, heading their separate ways; Eve on her way to the yard to slog, and Jane on her way to her lavish hotel to relax.

🕐 🕐 🕐 🕐 🕐

Three weeks later, Eve moved to the permanent ward; and having received the solicitor's letter confirming her share of the will a few days after having seen Jane, had left her assured that leaving the workhouse was merely a matter of time. She had been seeking employment in vain;

refused as a servant for lacking a reference, and outpaced by office jobseekers possessing more skills.

Sally had recovered from her epileptic fits, and was now back at work, having been freed from the hospital ward in a matter of days.

A few weeks after that, Eve took leave from the workhouse to travel with Jane to Newbury Heath, where together they viewed the house they would sell in due course; the former planning to buy an abode with her share. That afternoon, Eve journeyed back, not reaching the grounds of the workhouse until it grew dark.

The next morning, during her break, she went into the foyer to see more new inmates arrive; each newcomer waiting in line to be bathed and stripped of their clothes, before donning the workhouse attire they all had to wear on joining the ranks of the poor. A few seconds later, two new latecomers arrived - a sour-faced woman and a fractious, mad-looking girl just into her teens; faces that Eve had encountered somewhere before. When the woman saw her, she scowled, conveying the same signs of hate she had shown when Eve worked at Mrs Hart's home.

But the hatred no longer hurt, as it was clear to Eve that Miss Molloy and the unbalanced daughter she bore had been ousted from Mrs Hart's house, and had turned to the workhouse for want of somewhere to stay.

Eve calmly averted her eyes before turning away; the saying "As you give, you receive" entering her mind. She made her way to the kitchen to commence her shift with a broad, gleeful smirk, reflecting that Miss Molloy was now trapped in the plight Eve had found herself in a few months ago - a dark, endless tunnel without any opening or light.

Printed and bound by CPI Group (UK) Ltd, Croydon, CR0 4YY